The Black of the Room

Anna Stein

The Isolation Chamber (is) a translucent plexiglass dome measuring 7 feet in height, 9 feet in diameter, and 7 ½ feet at the base. It is surrounded on five sides by a system of fluorescent and incandescent lights by means of which the interior of the dome can be flooded with diffuse light of any intensity or wave length.

Toilet facilities, a food chamber, a two–way intercom system, and an air conditioning unit are all built into the floor of the dome, making it unnecessary of the (subjects) to leave the chamber for any purpose during the isolation period. A TV camera is mounted on the ceiling of the dome, making it possible to keep (subjects) under constant surveillance. The only piece of furniture in the chamber is an inflated air mattress on which the (subject) lies. Entrance to the dome is through a trapdoor in the floor which also serves as a food chamber.

The Isolation Chamber: *Intellectual Change During Prolong Perceptual Deprivation: Low Illumination and Noise Level.* John P. Zubek, M. Aftanas, J. Hasek, W. Samson, E. Schludermann, L. Wilgosh and G. Winocur (The University of Manitoba).

This research was supported by the Defense Research Board of Canada, Project No. 9425-08. <u>Perceptual and Motor Skills</u>, 1962, 15, 171-198. Southern University Press 1962. Monograph Supplement 1-V, 15.

The Black of the Room

CHAPTER 1

Six Weeks Earlier

That Spring day in 1958 was absolutely gorgeous. The air was warm and sweet with the scents of flowering crab apples trees and lilacs. The bright blue sky had an occasional wisp of cloud cross its surface. The sun was a bright, warm, golden globe. Sheila Pritchard saw the advertisement on the wall in the local YMCA when she went for her swimming lesson on Thursday.

> Recruiting male and female adults for scientific research in sensory area. Must be 21 to 45 years of age and in good health. A research fee of $250 will be paid to each participant who successfully completes the term of the first portion of the study (3 days and 3 nights). Contact: Maxwell Meddleton, PhD. for further information at GRIS 6365, between 9 am and 11 am Monday to Friday. Possible further earnings if accepted for more advanced research of slightly longer duration (up to seven days and nights).

The advertisement was still up. She had seen it in various locations and in different languages. She knew it was the same advertisement because the name and telephone number were always the same regardless of the language. Sheila had talked about the advertisement to Dennis's mother. It was great that she was willing to look after the children while she was involved in the first part, providing she met the criteria. She had also agreed to take Tony and Caroline if Sheila was accepted for the second part. If she was able to participate in both parts she figured she would have enough money to buy the golf clubs that Dennis wanted for his birthday. Wouldn't he be surprised? The clubs would be from her, Grandmother Pritchard, Caroline, and Tony. She had already managed to save four hundred dollars and Grandmother Pritchard had given her a hundred dollars so far. She didn't want her to give up any more of her savings as she knew her pension was not very large. Taking part in the research project sounded like it might be fun. It was already two o'clock so there was no point in calling today. She would call tomorrow morning while the kids were having their breakfast.

David Carter saw the same advertisement in the campus newspaper. He needed money. If the research could be done during his break from classes, that would be perfect. He had no classes from Thursday morning to late Tuesday evening. He really wanted to be a successful candidate. He had phoned last week and his interview with Dr. Maxwell Meddleton was scheduled for later in the afternoon, between his last two classes. He was looking forward to assisting scientific research. There had already been groundbreaking work carried out by other researchers out east. David was curious as well and he wanted to find out just what was involved. Would this work? Would it put River City College and Winnipeg on the map? The real reason, if he was honest, was the money. Money was important and he needed money. An engagement ring was being held for him. Kay was all that mattered to him.

Gunther Hiebert saw the advertisement in a Kirkfield Park grocery store window. He was unemployed. The money would be a lifesaver for him. He was sure he would get several free meals out of the deal. He looked at the clock on the wall of the grocery store. It was already ten to eleven. He decided to place his call from the payphone. Afterwards, he would inquire if he could make a few dollars by unloading stock or cleaning up the grounds outside the store. He would need to leave the number for the pay phone and a specific time to call him back and he would have to make sure to be in the store when the phone rang. He no longer had access to a home phone.

Carmen Aiello hadn't seen the advertisement herself but she overheard several people discussing the advertisement over coffee in the cafe she frequented. She had gone to a lot of trouble to look for the advertisement in the Italian paper.

Si cercano adulti (uomini e donne) per uno studio scientifico nei campo sensoriale. I partecipanti avranno I/etla 21 ai 45 anni e saranno in buona salute. Una quota di $250.00 sara pagata ciascuno dei partecipanti che completeranno con successo la prima parte dellow studio (tre gíorni e tre notti). Per informazioni ed interviste per determinare se siete adatti per tale ricerca, siete pregati di contattare il Dott. Maxwell Meddleton al GRIS 6365 dalle òre 9:00 alle 11:00 antimeridiane dal lundi ai venerdi. C'e la possibìlitia di guadagnare di piu se siete accettati per una ricerca piu approfondita che richiederebbe un periodo di tempo piu lungo (circa sette giorni e sette notti).

She wanted to get out of this one-horse town. The siren song of the west, otherwise known as Vancouver, had been luring her on a daily basis. She knew if she could just get away from Winnipeg her life would change. And, without a doubt, it would be a change for the better. She had money saved up. If she was accepted, the money would be the beginning of her emergency financial cushion. She did not anticipate any trouble finding a job and having extra money wouldn't hurt. She would need to find a place to live close to the University. Carmen had already made inquiries about attending evening classes. She intended to get a degree. Right now, she wasn't sure in what but she had time to decide that.

CHAPTER 2

Professor Maxwell Meddleton surveyed the stack of telephone messages. His latest advertisements had garnered a good crop of guinea pigs. His offer of two-hundred and fifty dollars for the first part, plus the fact the participants discovered that the first sessions were harmless, guaranteed little or no hesitation in getting agreement to the second part of the research session. What guaranteed their participation in session One was the offer of four-hundred dollars on completion of the second part, providing they were chosen. Max also came to realize that he had to refer to the experience as sessions not experiments. The word experiments brought on major hesitation from the participants. Session, on the other hand, appeared to be harmless and there was no hesitation regarding participation. It was all semantics. He now had an excellent cross-section of participants which included college students, housewives, government employees and even some medical types. He wished he could have had representation from the upper crust, where the money was. He was curious. Did financial excess guarantee a different breed of guinea pig? He knew obtaining their participation would have required a much sweeter pot. Unfortunately, the budget just would not take that kind of expense. His curiosity as to whether they would stand up better than the other participants, his ordinary citizens, would just have to be shelved for now. He had a good cross-section of human guinea pigs. It was all a matter of perspective or as he liked to think of it *sensory deception*.

Max was continually amazed at the gullibility of human beings. Surround them with the trappings of the situation and they would follow instructions without question. Maybe he was just fortunate enough to have only encountered the truly gullible, perhaps even stupid. But no, there were more than enough college grads as well as undergraduates. One would think they would be more suspicious, curious, or even questioning. He believed there was a correlation between human behavior and the behavior of lemmings. How much longer would he be able to keep the funding channels open and flowing at this current spending pace? The work was proving to be a gold mine. What had really taken off was the reaction of the human guinea pigs when the unknown was introduced in the total darkness of the second session. Then, their terror became a wide open, yawning abyss.

Up to the end of the first session they experienced up to a week of sensory deprivation with the lights on all the time. They did not experience any darkness. There was no night. The room temperature was constant.

For the second part, where they earned the remainder to make up the four-hundred dollars, they were exposed to twelve hours of light and twelve hours of complete darkness. It was during the twelve hours of darkness that the unknown was introduced through hidden locations in the floor, walls, and ceiling. Since he had adjusted the protocol for Session Two the sounds were usually sufficient, but the really tough buggers needed extra persuasion. That was when something cold, damp, or slimy would be introduced into the black that enveloped the participant. On occasion, an unrecognizable form would be found to be sharing the space and darkness with the subject.

His other persuaders even gave Max cause for discomfort, though he knew they were figments and would disappear before daylight broke or before the subjects regained consciousness if they ended up passing out. The amazing part was that even without windows, sunlight enveloped the fabricated pod like ocean water. Each subject was instantly aware when the sun began to rise. The black of the room became dark gray, then light gray, then instant brightness. The subjects became even more aware of time when the sun began to set. There was no need for adjustable lighting. Their reactions to the coming of darkness and its length of stay that was the most important aspect of the experiment, along with the surprises.

The shadows in the pod lengthened until the entire room was black as pitch. Max had been able to expose most of the human guinea pigs to the unknown for only one or two nights. Very few had made it to the third night and no one had made it past the fifth night, or even to the end of the week. He had left his subjects with the impression that they would have to last the full week to collect the four hundred dollars in full. If they fainted or passed out in the night then that was it for them. Their participation ended and there would be little or no money coming forth.

They were not allowed to bring anything in with them. No books, no writing materials, no flashlights, or radio. Their food, water, and clothing changes were delivered via a dumbwaiter. There was no contact with another human being for the duration that they occupied the pod. Every morning after breakfast, a set of questions would be placed in the dumbwaiter. The subjects answered these and put them back in the dumbwaiter for return to the lab. The subjects were observed in the daytime by the technicians but there was no contact. The pod was bare except for a toilet, sink, cot, and a sleeping bag. A covering of some sort for the night had to be provided. But the covering had to be safe from being used as an apparatus to harm oneself. He did not know how a participant would fashion an apparatus to hang themselves on, therefore, that wasn't a concern for him. Access to the toilet was unrestricted and there was a privacy screen that extended up about four feet. The toilet was hardly ever used during the nights of the second session. Its non-use was almost guaranteed with the appearance of the unknown and the fear factor kicking in. That was usually the end for almost all the participants --- the fear factor. That was the reason for the changes of clothing and the disposal of said soiled clothing. Max had the pod wired for sound, as well as heart rate and motion sensors in the walls, floor, and cot. The sensors were activated by any movement including screams, breathing, and/or heart rate. It would have been very illuminating to watch everything unfold every minute, but technology, unfortunately, was still behind. Soon though.. He was waiting to hear from a company that could film in the dark. And when he was able to purchase that piece of equipment he would have access to it all. Nothing would be secret. He would film his guinea pigs in the dark. They would not be able to keep anything secret because of the darkness. For now, though, he had to settle for the audio tapes of the nighttime sessions and the films of the daytime sessions.

Max's thoughts centered on his latest participants from the Session Two sets. They were his human guinea pigs or lab rats. Sheila, the wife of a City of Winnipeg constable, and David Carter, another very interesting individual and a brilliant student. Both had made it through the longest trial in the second session. Officially, both had only completed three nights but David had, in reality, completed four nights. Max had changed the protocol order for Session Two for David. There was no harmless first night. The fear factor had been introduced as soon as darkness had descended. David and Sheila had both collapsed into a vegetative state and their recovery on gaining consciousness was nothing short of amazing. Both were very calm when they were released to return home. Max would review the audio tapes and graphs from the second session later on. Kay, his senior technician, and his other assistant, Janice, evaluated the audio tapes and films from the daytime sequences of the first session. He had begun allowing Janice to view the daytime sessions of Session 2. He decided that he would run through the last of the applications over the next month. The next set would begin in about a week's time.

In about three months' time, the sensors would be removed from the pod walls, floor, and cot. The microphone, cameras and television would be removed and the pod would return to its original bare bones state. A room without windows on a floor that did not exist. He had already begun writing up his research paper but he was still undecided as to which journal he should submit it to. That would be a decision that would have to be made very carefully. He did not need any do-gooders with placards marching on college property, writing letters to the editor in the local paper or even appearing on any afternoon talk spots.

Max knew that Kay thought the Session 2 subjects should have been re-acclimatized to their normal environment over a much longer period of time. She felt they needed several days and not a couple of hours. It was amazing how embarrassed his human guinea pigs looked when they found out in the cold light of morning that there was absolutely nothing terrifying in the pod with them. Only their imagination, of course. He smiled as he remembered the bundle of rags with the oily covered ball attached that was tossed into the pod. That was the limit for the cop's wife. His earlier checks of the tapes revealed that. Somehow she had got past her demons and her breathing had settled down. He had known she would be fine. He had almost left to get himself some coffee when suddenly her heart rate had increased dramatically and she began keening. It was unnerving. He knew exactly when she lost consciousness. That was when he entered the pod. The lights were triggered and she eventually came to. He didn't dare leave her alone. He had ended up staying with her for the remainder of the night. She panicked if he dimmed the lights, even while he was in the pod with her.

Each subject brought several changes of clothing with them, along with a toothbrush, hairbrush, and soap. As soon as light began to envelope the pod they could obtain clean clothing from the dumbwaiter. They were also provided with a waterproof bag for their soiled clothing. The soiled clothing would be burned in the incinerator. They were all aware of this aspect because it was all included in the information package and instructions. "During the second session, any soiled clothing will be placed in a bag provided to you. Each morning, if you have a bag with soiled clothing, you can place it in the dumbwaiter and it will be incinerated. You will also have the opportunity to place the bag of soiled clothing into the incinerator yourself on your final morning of participation." For some reason that he could not fathom or understand, the subjects appeared to enjoy getting rid of their clothing. Some left with smiles, others with a jaunty step, and others chattered non-stop.

David Carter had been different. He had not wanted to close the door on the incinerator. He had complained that the hallway was too dark. It had floor to ceiling windows at either end. Sheila Pritchard, on the other hand, had handed her bag of clothing to the technician to dispose. She just wanted to get home to her children and husband. Her husband had been out of town and her children had been cared for by her husband's mother while she had participated in the second session. Max was sure that she would be fine. Her period of adjustment might be a little longer than it had been for previous participants, but she had lasted longer than most. She had almost outlasted David Carter.

Max wished that he could take his research further but he was running out of time. Even, now, his colleagues were poking around, demanding that the lab and observation area be made available for their scrutiny. Some were demanding a site visit while others wanted a research presentation in seminar format. Well, he was not ready for that yet. He had fought them at every turn. He was on his way. Scientific success would be his. He could envision interviews by national newspapers, major radio stations and maybe even the Canadian Broadcasting Corporation and its new thing, television! He would be as famous or even more famous than Milgram or Zimbardo! Max realized he was indulging in a daydream. Not a common occurrence for him.

He put the messages in a pile on his desk and got up to leave his lab office. He needed to make sure all was ready for the next participant. He could do that in the observation pod.

He had heard the elevator a little earlier but it had appeared to stop on one of the lower floors. Whoever had come in and used the elevator was not coming up to see him. He believed he was the only one still in the building at this hour. He caught a glimpse of his reflection in the darkened glass.

No sign of a pot belly. He still had all his hair and not a trace of gray. He played tennis and golf in the spring and summer and volleyball and hockey in the fall and winter. His five o'clock shadow was possibly his only conceit. Whether he was wearing his lab get up, business suit, or tux, he carried it off like a runway model. He smiled and winked at his reflection. He was still in A1 shape. No need for him to diet. He enjoyed his red meat but he was careful not to overdo it. He also enjoyed fish and salads. Desserts were not much temptation for him. His vice if he had one, he conceded to himself, was scotch, double malt and no less than eighteen years old. Expensive, but oh so worth it. The scotch sliding down his throat was similar in sensation to sliding across a beautiful, nubile naked female form.

Max heaved a great sigh. He wished he was already back at his apartment. He did not expend much serious thought on his male students other than he knew they were in awe of him. Yet he conceded to himself he did have another vice—his female students. He could not seem to keep his hands off of them. The prettier they were the harder it was for him. They adored him and he never had to have coffee or lunch on his own or with his colleagues unless that was his choice. He could be so understanding, an arm across their shoulders, a whispered confidence or remark, the accidental light brushing of fingers on a breast. This progressed to meetings off campus, drinks after hours, hand holding, and caressing of an adjacent thigh. It never took very long to get them into his bed.

He usually enjoyed the benefit of choice three or four times a year, depending on the crop. It had crossed his mind that Kay would make an excellent conquest but her work in the lab and pod was without comparison. She was better than the best, so why rock the boat? He would study his delectable students a little longer before making his choice. Of course, he always dropped them gently. His genius was the fact that they always thought that they had dropped him and that was the cherry on top. There was never any blow back on him. Max got himself a cup of coffee from the main lab and then turned the coffee pot off, locked the door behind him, and set off back to the observation room. He still had a couple of hours of listening to do and then he could head for his apartment.

He had been plagued by an uncomfortable feeling for most of the week. He wished he knew what was bothering him, especially tonight. He just could not account for it. He took the stairs to the observation pod. The sooner he finished checking the tapes, the sooner he would be able to leave and he promised himself a double scotch when he got back to his apartment.

CHAPTER 3

Deliver Us from Evil

Kay parked her car illegally in the loading zone. She prayed that the parking patrol was enjoying their coffee instead of driving around looking for cars that were illegally parked. She did not need another ticket. She had dozens in her glove compartment. She also did not need any kind of record of her visit to the building tonight. Kay fumbled in her bag for her building keys and as she turned to walk to the building she remembered she needed to lock her car. Car locked, head lowered to cut down on the painful bite of the wind that screamed round the building. "Damn." It was so cold the key did not want to turn. Kay realized that it wasn't the key. Her fingers were so stiff that her attempts to unlock the door were pathetic. Finally, the door unlocked and she moved inside. The doors wheezed shut behind her. The nighttime emergency lights provided the only illumination.

Suddenly she had to pee! There was no ignoring the tremendous bladder pressure and the shivers that ran down her spine and popped like flash bulbs in her nipples. The shivers were electric and painful. She pushed the heavy hallway door open with a furtive look around and made her way to the women's washroom. She chose the middle cubicle, slipped her bag over the toilet paper holder, and hung her coat on the door hook. The way her coat hung covered the crack in the door. Now, no one could see in. But really, she thought to herself, who else would be here at this time of night? Kay hiked her skirt up. With difficulty she peeled down the elastic of her tights and her panties. They had gotten tangled and rolled down together. She sat down just in time. It's a good thing she did not ignore the signals from mother nature. How could she be so cold on the outside and her pee be so warm as it leaves her body? She wished she could move some of that inner warmth to her fingers and hands.

She marshalled her thoughts while sitting quietly on the toilet. Should she take the stairs or the elevator? If she took the stairs she would have to stop part way to have the strength to finish the climb. The stairs would be the quieter approach. If she went all the way to the 6th floor with the elevator she would get there very quickly, but the noise would be the tip-off that someone else was on the floor. She decided to take the elevator to the third floor, then walk to the far end of the building and take the stairs the rest of the way up. She hated elevators! Taking the end stairway gave her the option of either one of two corridors. The one furthest from the lab would be best. The combination of stairs, elevator and farthest corridor would give Kay an advantage of several minutes and reduce the risk of bumping into Dr. Meddleton.

Her plan in mind, thoughts in order, Kay stood up and managed to unroll her underpants from her tights. She tugged them up. Then she pulled on the waistband of her tights. "Damn!" She's pulled too hard. She's ripped the crotch! "Another four seventy-five down the drain." She pulled her skirt down and tucked in her twin set. She shrugged into her coat and grabbed her bag and then remembered to flush. "Jeez!" She winced. Maybe she should have just left instead of flushing? She's made enough noise to wake the dead. She unlocked the cubicle. There was no time for hand washing. She opened the door to the hallway, and peered out, scanning the corridor. Nothing unusual. Out the door, around the corner to the elevator. She pressed the call button. "Hurry, hurry," she intoned under her breath. The elevator cables clunked and rattled, then the sensor went ping and the doors slid open. She scanned the compartment before entering.

"Let's get this over with," she whispered softly. Then stepped into the elevator and pressed the button for the third floor. The doors slid shut and the elevator rattled its way up to three. The cables made their usual noisy introduction before the doors began sliding open. Before she got off Kay decided to press the buttons for the basement and the second floor. Even if Dr. Meddleton was in the corridor instead of his office he wouldn't know who called the elevator. It would give her a few precious minutes if she was lucky. "No," she told herself sternly, "luck has nothing to do with this. It is all in the planning." Kay made it to the far stairwell, pushed open the door and started up the stairs. Dr. Meddleton didn't not know that she discovered the secondary entrance to the lab. The entrance that no one knew about, especially the participants.

Participants! What a laugh. By the time he was done with the people who signed up for the second part they were basket cases! The realization that their life would never be the same again would be a long time coming. Kay decided to use the secondary entrance. She'd wait for Dr. Meddleton to return to the observation pod, one room away from Hell!

Her breathing was normal. Everything was dead quiet. She reached the fifth floor. Her steps took her down the hall and into a secondary corridor on the left. She stood quietly and counted off the doorways in her mind's eye. There it was. The key was inserted. "Bloody Hell!" What a racket unlocking the door made. Kay opened the door, removed the key, and entered. The door closed behind her with a soft thunk. She should have had her flashlight ready. Finally her fingers tighten on the rubber wand. She pulled it out of her bag and clicked it on, a wavering wobbly light. She realized she is shaking. "Get yourself together," she told herself sternly. She hiked her bag over her shoulder and started up the iron ladder. She was holding the flashlight and the iron ladder supports. At the top she moved the trapdoor ever so slightly. "He's left a light on." She could not see into the entire room but he must have still been at the elevator, waiting to see who was coming in so late at night.

Gingerly and very quietly Kay pushed the trapdoor open. She lifted it out of the way and climbed up into the observation pod. She maneuvered the trap door shut and left the latch unlocked. She placed her coat behind the cabinet where it could not be seen. Her bag was dropped on top of her coat. The flashlight laid on a table. It made a muffled thunk! Kay stationed herself where she could not be seen, behind the door next to the big bookcase where she had a clear view of his desk and chair but he could not see her. She was counting on his not knowing that anyone else knew about the secondary entrance. He had told the other assistant that it was a ceiling access for the electrical trades. In reality, it was the emergency entrance in case any of the subjects went around the bend. Near as she could tell from the films she had been allowed to view, Dr. Meddleton only used the secondary entrance when he knew the participants were unconscious. These were the Session Two participants only.

So far, she had viewed two of the daytime Session Two films. The one Dr. Meddleton had shown her and the one Janice had shared with her. She knew she had pissed him off with her concerns about their well-being and the fact that there was no panic button for them to use. She had stopped voicing her concerns to him but her curiosity was definitely piqued. She had studied the film sequences very carefully. When she was preparing the pod for the participants she took time to look around, very nonchalantly, of course. She had not wanted to tip Meddleton off then and she did not want to tip him off now.

Kay put her hand in her skirt pocket and her fingers closed on a piece of metal about six inches long. She drew it out of her pocket, pressed the slightly raised piece on the handle. Quietly, a long thin steel blade shot out. It clicked as she locked it in place, louder than the silence of the room. Every detail had to be perfect. She knew Max would return to the observation section of the pod any minute. He probably wouldn't even be aware of her presence. She would have time to walk up behind him and...and...what? Slit his throat? Stab him in the back? His throat would be easier but very, very messy. All those British murder mysteries she read were good for something after all. If she went for his back then she would need to push the blade in hard enough to do immediate damage. She remembered an experiment with rats she had assisted with several years back. Spinal damage guaranteed non-movement. She certainly didn't need him trying to get up and attacking her. If she pushed the blade in at an upward angle that should do it.

What was that noise? Was he finally returning? "Please, let's get this over with," she muttered under her breath.

The door opened. It swung soundlessly into the room and the air pressure changed as the door whumped shut. His fingers enveloped his coffee mug. He looked distracted. His steps carried him across the room to his desk. He put his coffee cup down and pulled out his chair. Sitting down, he moved around in his chair until it felt right. The chair creaked several times. Kay observed all this from the corner and thought to herself that he should really get a new chair. But after tonight, he wouldn't need a new chair. She watched as he sipped his coffee. Max put his cup down, put on the headset, reached for the audio tape and the graph print-out. He switched the audio on and bent forward at his desk.

Kay moved soundlessly, the blade handle clenched in her fist. Someone should have done this long ago. What he has been doing might not be against the law, but it was definitely against God's laws, resulting in flawed, fragile, broken human beings, broken lives, shattered minds. Men and women who no longer believed what their brains told them. Men and women who would expect cruel treatment from family and friends. Men and women who would never trust anyone ever again; who could no longer tolerate darkness of any kind; who slept with the lights on all night long. Men and women who feared nothing about the dark before would awaken in a cold sweat, screaming, crying, even moaning continuously in their sleep. Men and women who had feared nothing much before were now afraid to be alone, and even more afraid to be with anyone, and their fear of the dark was beyond measuring. That was what Kay had noticed as each participant was preparing to leave. The aura of fear that each projected.

Kay had not encouraged David to offer himself as a subject. She had told him there had to be another way to get the money he needed. If only she had known he wasn't listening to her. He had only pretended to listen and then went ahead and enrolled without telling her. She had not even realized what he had done until she saw the daytime film sequences of the second session. Up to now all she had viewed were the sequences on film from the first session. She could imagine what the audio tapes for the night sessions would reveal. Kay did not know how she kept her revulsion and hatred hidden from Dr. Meddleton. He was usually very perceptive and unusually quick about picking up on signals and emotions. Maybe he did not pick up on hers because she was not a piece of celluloid. There was nothing to play back again, and again, and again. There was nothing to see in the dark. Max did not know she had already seen a filmed sequence of the second session.

Kay would never forgive him for destroying David, for

destroying what they had. For causing her to end up alone. Standing in the observation room, a knife clenched in her fist, she did not care if she died in the attack, nor if she was caught. David was gone. He was a shell of his former self. He did not know what he was doing. He had been looking for freedom from the demons, release from the hell his mind had imprisoned him in. Kay had searched for David. She had looked all over for him but she still had not been able to find him. Someone was going to have to file a missing person's report soon. Dr. Meddleton had to pay. David had seemingly vanished overnight. His absence was now a matter of concern for her.

She came up behind Dr. Meddleton and drove the knife into his back. She twisted it as she pushed it in. Then she yanked it out and again plunged the blade into the back of his neck. He tried to move, to get up, but she had shoved his chair forward when she drove the blade into his back. He was immobilized. The second strike, the knife into the back of his neck finished him off. His eyes were open but not seeing, his mouth was a perfect circle but no sound was coming from him. He slumped forward and his face hit the desk, spilling his coffee. Kay grabbed him by the back of his head. She held his perfectly cut hair in her fists and repeatedly smashed his face into his desk. Blood spurted from his nose and leaked from his mouth. She noticed pieces of marble white laced with pink and red. They were bits of his perfect teeth.

Kay pulled the knife out with a mighty yank! She wiped the blade clean on his shirt, pressed the button and the knife blade retracted. Kay shoved it into her pocket. She grabbed up her coat and slipped it on. She picked up her bag. Where was the flashlight? She glanced around and spotted it on the table, grabbed it and went over to the ladder and began her descent. It was taking so long to get back down. She did not care if she left her prints behind. After all, she worked for him and she worked in that room. Her prints would be all over the place along with the prints from all the other students who worked for Dr. Meddleton. Kay was responsible for cleaning and prepping the subject/participant pod and the observation room every time they were used.

"That was for you, David. Goodbye, my love." There was something wrong. She could not see. Everything was blurred. She realized she was crying. She had to stop this before someone saw her. She had to get herself under control. Tears were for later. She had to get back to her car and get the hell away. Kay used the far stairs again. This time running all the way down, into the hall, around the corner, and out the door. There was her car. Did it have a ticket? "No, not yet." She unlocked her door and threw her bag across the front seat. "Gotta get the hell outta' here." Security would be conducting rounds very soon if they hadn't already been by. She breathed a sigh of relief as her car started. She put it in reverse, backed up, and swung around, heading down the road. Kay drove within the speed limit even though all her nerves were screaming at her to drive faster. Her thoughts wandered from the task she had just completed. What would River College and the Psychology Department do now?

Kay drove and drove. She had no idea where she was

going. She just wanted to be far away. She knew that David was lost to her. She also knew that Dr. Maxwell Meddleton's days of destroying a subject's psyche were over and done with.

CHAPTER 4

Find the Light

It was bitterly cold on the Fortune Street Bridge. The winds picked up the street grit, whirling it around and hitting the exposed skin of anyone foolish enough to be out tonight. A body needed to squint to keep the grit from injuring one's eyes. Constable Pritchard trained the searchlight on the black water below the bridge. They would not be able to locate anything tonight. The current was a mess in this area. If anyone had taken a header over the side, the body would not surface for days. But, they had to try. It was their job. Another twenty minutes and they would have to give up and wait for morning. It was too dangerous for a dive team. They would be using grappling hooks and nets. Push down, drag, pull up. Free the debris or come up with an empty net. Push down, drag, pull up. Over and over. The two boats moved in tandem but the winds were making their efforts almost impossible to carry out. Pritchard leaned over the side of the bridge. No one was even sure what they were looking for. A driver approaching the bridge in a half-ton just before the power failure was sure he had seen something go over the side. He thought he'd heard a splash. No other noise. Just the wind and maybe a splash. He had found a pay phone and asked the operator to call the police.

Dennis Pritchard glanced down again. The grappling hooks and net were being pulled in. The search was over for tonight. "Thank God!" His ears were damn near frozen. Even his double thickness leather and wool gloves did not keep his fingers from stiffening up. The only part of him that had any semblance of warmth was covered by his buffalo hide coat. It weighed a ton but it was warm.

The search would probably be the lead story on the morning newscasts. He wondered how the body, if there really was one, would surface. Would it be found further down river by a fisherman? Would it wash up in the shore debris and be found by a resident walking their dog? Or would it get as far as the Lockport Locks? "Well," he thought, "there is no point in worrying about it now." He rolled up the cord for the searchlight and then reached up to remove the connection from the post. People were not even aware of the connection. It was covered by a dark, green movable plate. All he had to do to conceal the receptacle was slide the plate back down. All you were left with was a light post on the bridge. He was glad his shift was almost over. Glad to be going home where a reheated meal and a very patient wife would be waiting for him. Caroline and Tony would be fast asleep and he wouldn't see them until the morning. He was off until midnight the next day. Pritchard looked up. What was the chief doing here? The commander was with him as well.

"What's going on, Chief? Is everything okay?"

The chief stood still for a moment, then, squaring his

shoulders, he came forward towards Pritchard. "Constable Pritchard, I'm sorry, you need to come with me. They will be waiting for us at the hospital."

"What do you mean? Waiting for us? Who's at the hospital?"

"Dennis, I'm sorry, it's your wife. A passerby called the emergency in. He and his wife were out walking and they saw her in the window. She was cutting herself up. We're not sure if the ambulance got to her in time. The commander was working late and he wanted to come with me as well. Come on, man! Let's get going!"

Dennis Pritchard was in shock. His wife...cutting herself up? There must be some mistake! There was no one more levelheaded than his wife. She kept both of them grounded. She was his center point. He knew it was a mistake. It just could not be Sheila.

"Don't worry about the car, Dennis. I've arranged for someone to return it to the station garage." Pritchard sat in the front passenger seat. The siren was switched on and, lights flashing, the car made a U-turn on the bridge and headed for the General Hospital. Dennis could not seem to think, except to think it must be a mistake!

"Chief, what about Tony and Caroline?"

"They are fine, Dennis. Your mother is with them. We arranged for a car to pick your mom up and a couple of officers went into the house with her. She and the kids are back at her place. It would not have been good for you or them to see all the blood."

Dennis cried out as if he had been mortally wounded. To himself he prayed, "Dear God, thank you for keeping the children safe. Please let Sheila be okay. Dear God, please let Sheila be okay." It was like the comfort of the rosary, that single repeated prayer. "Let Sheila be okay - let Sheila be okay - be okay." He realized that he still had the searchlight in his hands, the cord was unbelievably tangled up. How could this be happening to him? Why was this happening? What had happened to Sheila? The car jerked to a stop in front of Emergency. Dennis jumped out and ran in. The commander was right behind him. The chief parked the car and followed them in, head bowed, steps slow. He too had no idea why this was happening. He hoped they could keep it out of the papers. This was the thirteenth unexplained suicide or similar event. He had at least two murders that did not make any sense whatsoever. Their investigations were still in the preliminary stages. He did not believe that there was a common thread. But, if there was, they had not found it as yet. He did not know if Sheila Pritchard had survived, would survive, or if she wanted to survive. He did not know what Dennis Pritchard was going to do. The chief thought about the rash of unexplained deaths, suicides and attempted suicides that were happening all over the city for no apparent reason. To date, only a couple of the suicides had been stopped before their successful conclusion. He wondered which group Sheila Pritchard was going to be in by morning. He would call for another car and leave this one for the commander, who was sitting with Dennis Pritchard. He also arranged for a priest to come and stay with Pritchard. That way, the commander would be able to leave if he wished. Pritchard had no other family except his mother, his wife, and the children.

Suddenly the chief was enveloped by an enormous wave of tiredness. No, not tiredness. He was exhausted. He would ask the nurse on duty to use the telephone. He could not remember the last time he felt so alone, cut off, so sick to death. Was the job getting to him after all this time? Maybe he should see his doctor and get some pills.

"Commander, I'm leaving. I've called for a car and a priest for Pritchard. Please make sure someone delivers him to his mother's home. I do not want him going into his house by himself. I'll arrange for a clean-up crew to go in first thing in the morning to remove all the traces. You can tell him he has the rest of the week off. He'll want to be here or with his kids. Here are the keys for the car we came in. I'll see you tomorrow." The chief swung around, headed down the corridor, out the door into the frigid night.

The commander took the keys that were proffered and watched as the chief disappeared through the swinging doors. If there was anything to be grateful for then it would be that Dennis had returned from the policing conference before this happened. He turned back to the room where Dennis was sitting with his wife. She had been sedated. Her cuts had been treated. Except for a somewhat serious facial cut, none of the others should leave any scars.

CHAPTER 5

Ten-thirty in the morning. The search team pushed the boats out into the water. Another pair of officers drove the trucks back up the hill with the boat trailer attached. No one knew how long they would be out on the water. It was a repetition of the previous forty-eight hours performed by the Water Recovery Unit. Push down, drag, pull up. How much longer would they have to keep this up before everyone gave up and just waited for the body? If there really was a body would it be close to the surface?

Bill Jessiman and his partner Matt Baxter were doing their job automatically, each thinking of Dennis and Sheila Pritchard. Word of her attempted suicide had spread through the ranks like a wildfire. Sheila had been admitted to the Psychiatric Ward of the General Hospital. She was still heavily sedated, her arms and legs crisscrossed with blade marks. She even had several cuts on her forehead and cheeks. Hell, a month ago they had all gone out to dinner together, Dennis and Sheila, Bill and Donna, and Matt and Bonny. Sheila was over the moon, she had managed to save enough money to buy Dennis the golf clubs he wanted. She had been so excited. She had not said where the money had come from. It had involved Dennis's mom babysitting while Sheila was away for a bit. Dennis had been out of town attending a Police Officers Association Conference involving members of law enforcement agencies from Canada, the United States and South America. He had wanted to take Sheila with him but the money was not available.

Matt Baxter was grateful he had no family close by. His wife had wanted to go with Sheila for the "free money" but no amount of money made up for his wife being away, by herself, without him. It wasn't that he did not trust her. He did. It was just that she was so gullible. Look how she fell for all his practical jokes. He remembered how she had been taken in with the "Bank Inspector Fraud". That one had almost drained their account. She had thought it was another of his practical jokes and had gone along with it. They still had not recovered the level of financial safety that they had prior to the fraud. Bonny felt the money for the first week as a volunteer for the research would make up for her gullibility. Matt was finally able to convince her that she was all he was concerned about. The money was missed but it was not going to ruin their marriage. And, if truth be told, it was all his fault because of all the jokes he played on her.

Now, they were taking turns with several other families helping Dennis and his mother. The old woman certainly had her hands full with two children under five years of age. He thanked the Lord the children had been kept safe from whatever had pushed Sheila over the edge.

Push down, drag, pull up. Push down, drag, pull up.

They had been at this for hours. "Whoa, what's that?" Baxter heard Jessiman say. Then—"Easy does it."

"Shit!" Baxter thought. "It's a body." Baxter and Jessiman very carefully tilted the net ever so slightly to form a loose basket around the waterlogged form. They did not want to lose it. Very carefully, the boats were put in reverse and they headed back to shore. Matt Baxter and Bill Jessiman would have been surprised to learn that their thoughts were nearly identical.

The coroner would be notified. He would have to come down and do an initial examination, then the poor stiff would be bagged, wrapped, and taken to the morgue. The autopsy would be done within the next day or two. Well, at least it appeared that the fish had not done too much damage to the poor sod's face. Both wondered if enough of the fingertips would be left to assist with identification. This guy had not been in the water for that long, maybe a week but no more than ten days. What was surprising was that the body had not turned up further downstream, closer to the Lockport Locks, or even snagged by the shore debris which would have made decomposition even worse.

"Sure is weird." Bill Jessiman voiced his thoughts aloud.

"What's weird?" Matt asked.

"How come the body stayed as close as it was to where it went over?" was Bill's reply. They had reached the shore and soon he and Matt would be done. The body had been carted away to the morgue. Their shift was really over and they could both head for home. It was a toss-up as to who was the luckiest this week. He and Jessiman, or the guys who pulled the murder detail at River College. He had been told that it had been awfully rank. The body had sat, undiscovered, the entire weekend and was not officially discovered until Tuesday afternoon when the afternoon research group reported to work. The students from Monday and Tuesday morning had not entered the lab. It had been locked so they had waited around and finally left. No one had thought to report anything to anyone. Wasn't that just like students or even anyone for that matter? No one was here, oh well we get some time off.

Bill Jessiman remembered his time in Teachers College. The obedience mentality. The unquestioning deference to authority. That was why, when graduates went out to teach, they could instill that same mentality in their students. They had firsthand experience. He guessed he could understand why Monday's students did not question the professor not being there or the lab not being open. It just meant a day off for them. Maybe they had been slightly inconvenienced but who cared about inconveniencing students. It was the Tuesday afternoon research assistant who had arrived after everyone else had been waiting around. She had a key and unlocked the door. She had stepped aside so that the others who were waiting could enter. Then all hell had broken loose. He wished he could be part of the murder investigation. There was no way that would happen until he passed his Sergeant's Exams. Bill was going to attempt the exams again at the end of the month. He hoped that the saying "third time lucky" was true. He had tried to convince Matt Baxter to have a go at the exam but his powers of persuasion were limited. If he passed the exam this time then duties like the one he had just finished would be a thing of the past. He certainly would not miss river retrieval patrol. If he passed the exam then an assignment like the River College murder would be a reality.

Bill had heard rumors of audio tapes that were almost impossible to listen to. Apparently, there were no visuals, at least not yet. It was definitely not true that what you don't know cannot hurt you. Whatever those poor saps had been put through it must have been gawd awful! Bill had two years of Teachers College and four years of teaching behind him. As a career choice it had proved to be a bust. If it wasn't asshole administrators, then it was overprotective, lax parents who were the bane of his existence back then. For the few students who would really achieve something, the lackadaisical attitude of the majority was no encouragement for any teacher. Police work was definitely better. There was something about the uniform that commanded deference and respect. Maybe it had something to do with the revolver. Who knew? All he knew for sure was that this was the job for him and it could be his career, his life even.

Bill checked his mail slot for messages before he left for home. He had not bothered to change out of his uniform. There were three messages from the Assignment Sergeant. He knew he could not leave for home until he found out what they were about. It must be important for him to have left him three messages. He crumpled them up and put them in his pocket as he strode down the hall and pressed the button to call the elevator. Inside, he pressed five, the doors slid shut, and a couple of minutes later opened up again on the fifth floor. Bill Jessiman took a deep breath and then knocked on the door.

A voice called out, "Come in." The sergeant was standing by the window. "Oh, good, Jessiman, it's you. I wondered if you had forgotten to check for messages. I really did not want to have to send a car to bring you back here."

Jesus, Bill thought, what the hell have I done? "Sergeant, I had river retrieval duty with Matt Baxter. We retrieved a body. We had to wait for the coroner to show up to take custody of the corpse. Then everything had to be cleaned up and put away."

The sergeant cracked a small smile. "Relax, Jessiman, you are not in any trouble. You are being reassigned for the time being to the River College murder. I know this is a bit unusual with your not having written your sergeant's exam yet, but I have every faith that you will be successful." Jessiman was stunned and realized he better be paying attention.

"It seems the River College population is somewhat different from the ordinary population. I think the PhD or college mentality may be the problem. I'm not sure why, but Detective Jimmy Moore believes your teachers training and teaching experience will prove to be an asset to the investigative team. You'll report to Detective Moore tomorrow morning at eight. I don't know whether he will want you in uniform or in plain clothes so come prepared for either situation. In addition, I want you to prepare a report which you will submit to me on a weekly basis until this assignment is completed or you are reassigned. I know you will think the reporting is an imposition, as in pain in the ass, but I believe it will benefit you when you write your exam. Right now, let's plan on meeting every Thursday at six pm to discuss your report. Also, don't forget to keep your notebook up to date. It is your most valuable tool in any investigation, especially when you are called into court as a witness."

Jessiman knew that this was very true. His first time in court, his notebook had saved his ass. He made sure he kept meticulous records. Some guys relied on memory. Not him. No sirree. In case he ever ran short, he kept a supply of a dozen or so in his sock drawer and another half dozen or so in his locker here at the station. When he was getting close to the end of one notebook, he would pop another into his pocket. If he forgot to pick one up when he was home the ones in his locker were there for when he was getting ready to go on shift.

CHAPTER 6

Five Weeks Ago

Professor Maxwell Meddleton had done his initial research into Sensory Deprivation along the same lines as colleagues at McGill, Duke, and Harvard. The subjects were kept in a totally dark room for several days at a time. The room had a panic button which, if used, would halt that particular session for the participant. They endured continual, constant darkness all day and all night. The subjects were tested before and after their time in the Black Room. There was also the set of questions they found in the dumb waiter every morning that had to be answered. Their measured feelings as opposed to perception were also recorded. The twenty-four-hour lights on component never appeared to stress the participants. If they appeared to be experiencing difficulties it was with being able to fall asleep with the lights on. Their own solution ended up with them covering their heads when they wanted to fall asleep.

Max had already reviewed the published papers of Milgram and Zimbardo. He had decided that his research protocol needed some tweaking. Max decided he would measure hearing and feeling and to some degree he would also measure perception. His subjects would occupy the pod for the daylight hours. Their reaction to the imminent descent of darkness and the time spent in actual total darkness as in nighttime would be recorded and measured. His technicians and student assistants could supervise and record the daytime observation sessions.

He, Dr. Max Meddleton, would supervise and record the night sessions. This time, unknown to the participants, there would be no panic button. The subjects would be advised that their reactions, and as well their reaction time, was being recorded and measured. In the event of evidence of discomfort displayed by the subject, which the sensors would reveal, he alone would enter the pod and the scientific endeavor would conclude for that subject. Max would chat with the subjects until the time was up and all lights were back on. The subjects never saw him enter the pod. He was already there when they became aware of their surroundings and he stayed with them until the technicians or assistants arrived in the morning to begin their work. He considered this time with them their debriefing period. In the morning, showers were accessed, clothing was replaced as necessary. Whether or not they chose to watch their clothing being incinerated was up to them.

The method for recruiting subjects would be different this time as well. There would be no recruiting by word-of-mouth. He had to ensure that no passing of information took place. Max also felt that the subjects needed to have a higher-than-average intelligence. However, he disagreed with his counterparts over the intelligence of the ordinary citizen versus the university or college student. Most other researchers believed that the most promising and accurate results would be obtained from college or university graduates. Max, on the other hand, believed if the interview progress was carefully carried out he could uncover those human guinea pigs with a better than average intelligence. Ordinary people did not have a lower intelligence than college or university students. By not using word-of-mouth recruitment methods, Max believed his results would be truer and more definitive because then the end result of the research period could not be influenced by prior knowledge.

Max was curious about a number of things. First, he wanted to find out if colour or lack of it, as in darkness, impaired judgment. Second, if sensory deprivation could adversely affect the intellect. Third, would there be a definitive loss of concentrative powers as in delayed or damaged thoughts. Fourth, could any of the parameters be affected or influenced by fear. And, finally, would any of the subjects experience hallucinations—or could hallucinations be induced using present circumstances in the pod—and if so, to what degree. Dr. Maxwell Meddleton, researcher extraordinaire, believed the answers to the questions he posed would place him at the pinnacle of scientific success. He believed the fear component he would be introducing to his next set of subjects would ensure the success that had so far eluded him. His name would be synonymous with Milgram and Zimbardo.

Dr. Meddleton had written up grant proposal after grant proposal. He was able to start the money train with the Department of Defence (Canada). It was many months before he learned the actual source of the monies he was receiving—an American Naval Research Unit via the Canadian Department of Defence. The Americans wanted to see if his results could be applied to quarantine, solitary confinement, interrogations and/or submarine duty situations. Hell, as long as the cash kept coming they could apply his results anyway they wanted.

The pod was constructed to specifications drawn up by Dr. Meddleton. A translucent Plexiglas dome measuring seven feet in height and nine feet in diameter. The base of the pod was seven and a half feet. The sides of the pod held fluorescent and incandescent lights. The interior could be flooded with any intensity or wavelength of diffuse light. A two-way intercom system and closed circuit television monitor were part and parcel of the set up. The food delivery system was via a dumb waiter. There was a cooling unit built into the floor to keep beverages cold and it was accessed from beneath when it required restocking. The subjects were totally unaware of the sliding panel. In addition, there was a toilet and hand washing station situated several steps down and behind a screen. The floor of the pod had been reinforced to accommodate air-conditioning tubes which ran silently. For daytime observation, the black and white closed-circuit television was mounted in the ceiling which provided constant visual surveillance. There were sensors built into the cot, walls, and the floor of the pod. Entrance for the subjects was via a trap door and ladder.

CHAPTER 7

Sheila Pritchard had sailed through the first portion of the Sensory Deprivation session. She did not believe she had slept very much but she had never felt so rested. The second part of the session was scheduled to begin the day after Dennis left for his Police Association Conference. Dennis's mom would look after the kids and when she was done with the second session, the golf clubs would be paid for. Sheila had arrived at the lab and had been walked through the steps by Janice, Dr. Meddleton's student assistant. She was informed at the end that for this portion there would be no panic button to access. Sheila was not worried. Dr. Meddleton would be there watching and looking after the recording devices and keeping an eye on things. After all, what could go wrong? The first part had been a snap! Sheila intended to get through and past three days and three nights. She was determined to earn the full four hundred dollars for the second part.

The first day was what she would call weird. She felt like she had slept for days. She had lazed about on the cot, had several drinks, a sandwich, and had also used the toilet and wash up facilities. She noticed the pod was becoming darker. At some point as the shadows lengthened Sheila realized that her apprehension was increasing. She did not know why. It would have helped if she could have talked to herself. Listening to what she was saying out loud might have helped. But talking out loud was not permitted. She wasn't about to lose the money. Instead, she admonished herself in her head. She got through the first night of the second session. Everything was fine. The second day was a repeat of the first one except there were tests to be done. The second night was more of a stretch. Sheila knew there was something in the pod with her but she could not see what it was. At one point, she brushed the floor with her hand and froze. How she managed not to scream her fool head off amazed her. Whatever had been on the floor was slimy and strand-like. She kept checking the cot to make sure whatever it was it could not invade the island that was her cot. She breathed a sigh of relief when she noticed it was getting lighter in the pod. Day Three was beginning. She got through all the tests and even managed a bit of a snooze. "Oh my God! It's getting dark!" The light was fading quickly. Sheila was scared. The "whump, whump" of her heartbeat echoed in her head and appeared to reverberate off of the pod walls. Dr. Meddleton would be there watching and looking after the recording devices and keeping an eye on things. She could do this. She would do this.

Sheila was not going to move off of the cot. She was not going to put her hands over the side of the cot. She would lie perfectly still and carry on a conversation with herself in her head. They could tell them that they could not talk or sing out loud but they could not stop her from talking to herself in her head. Dr. Meddleton had no control over that. Sheila was stretched out on the cot when she heard a soft whoosh, so quiet that she almost missed it. Now, it was too dark to see anything, but something was in the room with her! She just knew it. Sheila lay on the cot, stiff as a board, her heart pounding, trying to control her ragged breathing.

Dear God, please help me. Give me strength to fight the devil in this room. She heard herself moan. She screamed silently. *No, I must not fall apart! I have to last! Last for at least four days and nights. I have to get the money. Dear God...Jesus Christ...Blessed Virgin... help me! Help me! What was that? There is something on the cot! Where did it come from? What is it?* Sheila sat up with difficulty and moved her hand to the foot of the cot. She felt a rounded shape. It was soft and attached to a wrapped bundle.

A baby! Where had it come from? How did it get into the pod? She inched her way down the cot and picked up the soft, squishy form. She cupped its perfectly rounded shape. Her fingers tried to find the eyes, nose and mouth. *Dear God, it doesn't have a face! Where is its face? God help me!* Sheila knew her control was slipping. There was nothing she could do. She flung the shape away. Sheila heard the splat when it hit the wall. She fainted.

Sheila came to very gradually. Dr. Meddleton was with her. The lights were back on. There did not seem to be anything else in the pod except Dr. Meddleton and her.

• • •

Max had just realized his evening was kaput! He would have to stay and talk with Sheila for the few remaining hours of the night.

She asked him, "What happened to the baby? What had happened to its face?"

Max's voice was filled with sympathy and concern. "My dear Mrs. Pritchard. A baby? There was never any baby of any age in the pod with you. I believe you may have been experiencing a hallucination. I almost entered the pod to assist you several hours ago but I did not because you appeared to have calmed down. Then the sensors went crazy. I thought there might have been a malfunction. By the time I realized there was nothing wrong you again appeared to have calmed down. You remember in the initial instructions if I have to enter the pod before the time is up your participation is at an end. I was trying to be fair. Then the sensors went wild again. They were so erratic I had no idea where you were in the pod. I really did think it was a malfunction. By the time I found out there was nothing wrong with the sensors you had fainted dead away. It has taken me awhile to revive you. Are you sure you are fine now?"

"Yes, Dr. Meddleton. As soon as the technician gets here I would like to use the shower facilities. The technician can toss my clothing into the incinerator. I just want to go home."

Max smiled at her. He had practiced his kindly, avuncular smile for weeks until he had perfected it. "No problem, Mrs. Pritchard, the technician and her helper will be in shortly." He smiled once more. "Do you think we can talk some more about your experience? I'm really not sure if you were truly hallucinating or not. Can you describe your thoughts and feelings in a bit more detail? You know, you were exceptional in carrying out the instructions. You did not talk out loud or sing or hum for the entire period in the pod. Truly you have amazing willpower. By the way, here is your cheque." Sheila took the cheque from his hand and stuffed it into her pocket without even looking at it.

"Willpower, schmelpower." Max knew exactly when she lost it. The readings from the sensors would be a gold mine. He could not wait to analyze the data. He checked his watch. The technician would arrive in about twenty minutes to half an hour. "Would you mind being on your own for a few minutes, Mrs. Pritchard?"

A panicked look flew across Sheila's face. "If you don't mind Dr. Meddleton, I do not want to be left alone. Please don't leave me. Don't leave!" she wailed.

"It's okay Mrs. Pritchard, I won't leave you until the technicians get here." In his head Max was boxing her ears. *Jesus! What a fucking baby.* He was going to have to see if his lab assistant and helpers would be able to come in earlier. These, *you're going to fine* sessions were such a drag and a real waste of his time. Max felt Sheila Pritchard had stretched his patience to the limit.

Max had an interview arranged for the following afternoon with Gunther Hiebert. He was not sure if Gunther would be satisfactory candidate. He was a silent stolid character except for all his questions. The dope was the sort that might cause him real trouble and probably real aggravation. He needed to review the Hiebert data and his answers to the test questions that he had completed. Hiebert sure had really meaty hands. He felt that they could inflict grievous injury without too much effort. Why was it the slow, stupid ones were the ones who ended up being the smart ones? Gunther had asked the sort of questions Max had expected from a university or college MA or PhD participant. He would decide tomorrow after he had reviewed his data. Right now, all he wanted to do was sleep.

Carmen Aiello had endured absolute hell for her four hundred dollars.

She sailed through the first part just like everyone else. The second session in the pod was a whole other story. Carmen had laid down on the cot as the night darkness began to envelop the pod. She was surrounded by blackness. She decided to keep her eyes squeezed shut until the warmth of the sun's days permeated the pods panels. As the shadows in the pod lengthened she took to her temporary bed and laid there, eyes squeezed shut and stiff as a board. According to the sensors, her pulse was taking off. Carmen only lasted two days and one night. She had not realized that she would receive the entire four hundred dollars. Carmen had believed she would have to last the whole week to collect. She witnessed her clothing being incinerated. She was glad that any permanent reminder of her time in the pod had been destroyed. She had taken four showers her first morning at home, not counting the two showers at the lab. She had also taken to sleeping with the lights on when she went to bed. Would these silly behaviors never end? She was packed and ready to go. The tickets for Vancouver were sitting in her purse. She could not wait to get going. Her level of excitement rose as the departure date came to be. The trip was about thirty-six hours. Two days and one night. She felt she could handle that.

The prairies were so flat she slept through them. The train was through Alberta. Next was British Columbia, but first they had to get past the mountains. Carmen could not wait. "Oh my God! Who turned off the lights?" Those were Carmen's last coherent thoughts. The depth of the darkness knew no end. Carmen shrivelled into herself. The train came out of the tunnel and into the light. The conductor and the other staff on the train were trying to locate the source of the banshee-like screaming that had stood everyone's hair on end. No one saw Carmen. Her body curled into itself, her eyes squeezed shut. She became aware of the sun's rays beating on the windows. She had no sooner opened her eyes and begun to uncurl her length when the train entered another tunnel. Carmen fainted. She had tried to scream but all that had emerged was a choking sound. Spittle trickled from the side of her mouth. Carmen was carried off the train on a stretcher when it arrived in Vancouver. She was breathing but no one was able to revive her. Her entry to the Emergency Ward was the prelude for the Psychiatric Ward of Vancouver General. She would be there for a long time.

CHAPTER 8

Max had enjoyed an excellent night. He awoke refreshed and full of vigor. He had reviewed his data on Gunther Hiebert. Max knew Gunther needed the money but Max couldn't put the memory of Gunther's large meaty hands out of his mind. He kept thinking those hands were Gunther's weapon. Max did not ordinarily entertain feelings of concern or empathy for his human lab rats but something about Gunther kept him on edge. He decided he would give him one-hundred and fifty dollars out of his own pocket. He felt something for that guy. He just didn't know what or why.

Gunther met with Dr. Meddleton. He needed the money. He would do or say whatever was necessary to get in on the second session. He sat in the outer office cracking his knuckles. The door to Max's office opened and Max called him in. Max ended up wasting an hour of his very valuable time explaining the criteria required for the second session. He used his practiced, perfect smile as he walked Gunther to the door. "Your involvement in the first part is greatly appreciated, Gunther. I know you need the money. I regret

I cannot use you for the second session. I want you to take this. It's not what you would have received for the second session but it should help you out some. I'm sure you can earn some extra money assisting other researchers. I'll give you a number you can call." Max stood in the doorway and put an envelope in Gunther's shirt pocket. Max shook Gunther's hand and wished him "good luck".

Gunther left Max's office and walked down the hall to the elevator. He put his hand to his shirt pocket and drew out the envelope. He opened it up and smiled as he counted out one-hundred and fifty dollars. He was no longer put out. He put the cash in his wallet and then put his wallet in his front pants pocket to deter would-be pick pockets. He strode to the main thoroughfare of the college grounds to catch a bus. Gunther rode the bus back to the city center. He would be able to buy himself a decent meal for a change. He knew he'd be okay. That Dr. Meddleton was an okay fellow. Gunther was glad he hadn't told him that he had been thinking of bowing out. Gunther rode the bus, staring out the window, thinking about how he would spend his money, cracking his knuckles the whole time.

Max had decided on his last participant for this last run. He would call David Carter in. David had already completed the first session. The data Max had reviewed looked good. He dialed David's number and the ringing was cut off in mid-ring. "Hello, David Carter speaking."

"David, this is Max Meddleton of River College. I understand that you are available from Thursday morning to Tuesday afternoon for the final Session Two run. That time frame is great as it fits in with the observation time I have available. You would occupy the Sensory Deprivation Pod for five nights. The session would begin at eight am on Thursday. How long it lasts is entirely up to you. Are you still willing to participate? Don't worry if you are having second thoughts. If you've changed your mind, it is quite all right." Max hated to give the withdrawing reassurance but he had to. He'd only had a half dozen or so subjects withdraw up to this point.

David was quite excited. "Sure, no problem. I have a date for the weekend but I'll postpone it. I'll see you Thursday morning at eight."

Dr. Meddleton and his other technician, Janice, met David when he arrived Thursday morning. David knew Kay wouldn't be there because she had classes. She was annoyed with him because he had cancelled their date for the weekend. He told her to use the concert tickets and to go with a friend. He promised he would make it up to her. He had not seen or talked to her in person, instead, he had left a message for her on her locker in the College. The concert tickets had been left in an envelope for her with the housemother of the residence. David knew she would be really annoyed. No, she'd probably be really, really angry. He had been so secretive for the last couple of weeks.

Kay had to put in time at the lab. She had not intended to work this weekend. David had stood her up. Well, technically, he had not. He had let her know that he had to cancel their entire weekend so now, she would be in the lab. She needed to review the audio tapes for the last couple of days of first session testing. Kay wished that Dr. Meddleton would allow her and the other technicians to review the data from the second session. Up to this point in time, she'd only talked to the subjects after their stay in the pod for the second session was completed. She had raised her concerns with Dr. Meddleton regarding their obvious fragile state when they emerged from the pod at the completion of the second session. Kay felt that Sheila Pritchard needed to be re-evaluated and even watched. She did not think that Sheila had emerged unscathed.

Dr. Meddleton had just poo-pooed her concerns. "Don't worry Kay, she'll be fine. A couple of weeks at home and she'll forget all about Session Two. She participated in this of her own free will and she got paid for her participation. She wanted that money. Actually, they all want the money. Even that ham-handed fellow, Gunther, that I told you about. The one I did not feel comfortable with taking part in the second session. He scared me."

Kay was amazed. Dr. Meddleton had never, never admitted to any misgivings before. She remembered that Dr. Meddleton had said he had given Gunther some money and she asked, "So why did you give him money?"

"Well, he was unemployed and he did need the money. At least that way I would not have to worry about him coming up behind me one night when I'm on my way home. I even gave him the phone number to register if he was interested in participating in other research."

Kay was astounded. Was Dr. Maxwell Meddleton

finally having second thoughts about his work and its effect on his subjects? Kay had brought her lunch with her. She would begin reviewing the audio tapes from the first session. There were also limited portions of film to review from the daytime for Session Two that made up the first part of the work. She sat down and put the first tape into the machine. She jotted down the name without thinking: David C, age 24, biochemistry major. She assigned him the next number, DB62. Kay froze. She stared at the name on the tape and the name she had written down. She realized whose name she had written down. "Oh God, David why did you do this? Why couldn't you believe me when I said it wasn't a good idea?" Kay knew that the harmlessness of the first session was the carrot on the stick that guaranteed participation in the second session. It was the second session portions that concerned her the most. She could not tell David why he should not participate but she thought her reservations would be sufficient to keep him from participating. "Davey, Davey." She said his name under her breath. "It's the second part of Meddleton's work that I was worried about. There's something not right about it. Davey, I don't want to lose you." Kay could not know that her worrying was all for nothing.

David arrived at Meddleton's lab on Thursday morning. After he went through the preparation phase and the talk that Max always gave the participants he was led to the ladder and trapdoor entrance. David climbed up the ladder through the opened trap door. He paused and looked around.

Max talked to him from the bottom of the ladder. "David, if you move into the pod, you will see the dumbwaiter. Right now it is open but once we get started the only time you will be able to access it will be for food, drinks, and changes of clothing. Why not have a look at it?" Max spoke as he was climbing up the ladder after David.

David was still looking around. Max pointed out the partition hiding the toilet and washbasin and the sleeping bag, rolled up along one side of the pod. He showed David the variety of beverages in the cooler. There were cold drinks including iced tea and a vitamin concoction made up especially for Session Two. For some reason, none of them ever appeared to enjoy the vitamin shake that was an alternate choice and it was not the drink of choice. They only got hot drinks with their meals.

"The dumbwaiter will only open up if there is food or drinks or clothing. You don't have to call out that you need anything. I will be doing the observation every night that you are here. My technicians will be doing the daytime observations." The delivery platform of the dumbwaiter was too small to support or hold a person and thereby did not allow a means of escape from the pod.

Max had decided David would be his final subject for this session of testing. He needed a break before he started up with the last set of subjects. He decided to increase the pace of this, his last session. Instead of introducing the unknown to David Carter and the others on the second or third night of the session, Max had decided he was going to introduce the unknown right off the bat on the first night. David's IQ was almost at the genius level. To date, Max had not tested anyone with as high an IQ as David. Max believed the results would prove to be significant.

CHAPTER 9

Session Two: Inside the Black Room

<u>Night 1</u>
Suddenly David was wide awake. He tried to see in the dark. What had awakened him? He lay on the cot listening to the darkness with all his might. He was as stiff as a board. What had woken him up? Was the cot moving? David sat up. He used his arm to lever himself to a sitting position. His hand and fingers splayed on the floor supported him. Suddenly, he felt something! *Jesus, what's that?* He could not see. It felt like cold scum. He shook his hand to try and rid himself of the stuff. Instead, some of it hit him in the face. He flinched and leapt off the cot. There was no place to go. He couldn't see anything. He moved forward slowly until he reached a wall. He would stay away from the cot. Now, he realized he had no place to go. No safe place. He was going to have to stay awake. He could sleep in the daytime. He moved along the perimeter. He needed to concentrate on something, anything, except what might be waiting for him in the dark. He would recite his biochemistry formulas in his head. He stopped in mid-thought. Was that a breeze? Where would a breeze be coming from? A minute or two later he realized

that the breeze was gone. He took another few steps, still skirting the perimeter of the pod. David choked off his yell. Something had just brushed against his face. God, it felt awful. It was like tentacles. Long and slimy! He jumped back. He was going back to the cot. He would pull the sleeping bag over his head. He'd hold the top shut with his hands above his head, like when he was a small boy.

David drew up his legs in the sleeping bag.. He was holding the top of the sleeping bag with both his hands. His legs shot out beneath him. He wanted to run but he could not. Whatever was out there was lying across the top of his sleeping bag. It had brushed against his fingers. David could only think of snakes. He was terrified of snakes. The shape moved as if to come in through the top of the sleeping bag. David fainted.

Max smiled ruefully, well that would be it for several hours. He would check up on him but he knew David would be just fine. He had been surprised by the sudden shout from David but that was the only sound he had made. Now, he was passed out. He wanted him for more than one night or part thereof, so David would be left to recover on his own. He'd wake up thinking that he had had a very bad dream. Max knew he had a few hours grace, so he set the alarm and made himself comfortable on the sofa.

The alarm went off. Max sat up. He rubbed the grit from his eyes. He checked the recording tapes. According to the peaks on the graph David was awake. He pulled on the tape to see if he could see exactly how long David had been awake for. It would appear that it was about forty-five minutes. Sunrise wasn't for another two hours. What could he be doing to pass the time? He checked the sensors to see if David had remained on the cot, or if he was stretching his legs. Suddenly, Max became alarmed. David was attempting to escape the pod through the trap door. He had to be stopped. Max pressed a lever. A small opening appeared on either side of the panels above the trap door. Each opening contained a large flask that was set in motion to tip its content. The contents of the flask was thick and somewhat mucous-like. Max had to divert David. He saw David's hands reach out to trace the opening of the trap door. He was looking for the slider locking device, the bolt. Instead, he encountered a substance that felt like thick gravy or maybe blood. David gave a strangled yell and threw himself sideways. He was sitting on the far side of the pod, holding his knees, his body bent forward, his knees clasped to his chest. Max could hear something. It took him several minutes to figure out what David was doing. The idiot was praying! Did he really believe prayers were going to help him? Max waited until David's breathing had settled down. He didn't want him to have a seizure or go into cardiac arrest while on the premises. He needed to be very careful. David was going to be a winner! Max just knew it. He felt it in his bones and his bones were never wrong! His bones also told him that David had been through enough for one night. It would be daylight soon. His technicians would be in to run David through another series of tests. Max figured that

David would sleep through most of the daylight hours. Max could hardly wait for the second night.

Max was wrong. David did not sleep. Janice, the technician, thought he was asleep several times but then his heart rate would take off and David would leap off of the cot in an absolute panicked state. Janice could not understand what was happening with David. None of the other participants had reacted the way he was behaving. Usually, she would arrive in the morning and signal the subjects to begin the tests which were activated with the press of a button. In between tests, the subjects always slept most of the day away. Neither Janice nor Kay had ever observed any of the night sessions. By the time either of them arrived in the morning the subject had usually eaten breakfast and changed clothes if necessary. If Dr. Meddleton was in the pod with them then Session Two was finished for this subject. The participants could also be in the office with Max. Max was usually at his desk and the subject was asleep on his sofa.

Janice made sure that David had completed the series of tests that he had to do. There wasn't much space on the form but Janice decided to make a note of David's behavior. She believed her observations were important. In her notes David was referred to as DB62. His wildly fluctuating pulse rate, his erratic behavior, the non-sleeping were all recorded. Her shift was over. Janice replaced all her materials and testing materials. She had indicated on the graph where her shift ended. That way, there would be no doubt as to when the later afternoon/early evening readings began. Janice noted that David's readings were not stable. The graphs showed many, many peaks and only a small area of calm indicated by the smallest peaks and a somewhat flat line appearance. Janice wanted to talk about this to someone. She knew Dr. Meddleton would rip a strip off of her. She decided to leave a message for Kay. Janice felt better just thinking about discussing these details with Kay.

Night 2

David completed the tests. They were so easy. He really could not decide what the actual point of the work being conducted was. He figured he'd had one gawd-awful nightmare. He remembered trying to locate the trapdoor bolt and after that there was nothing. The sun was still shining and the pod lights were on. The light was beautiful!

David nodded off a couple of times but in no time at all the shadows in the pod began to lengthen. Soon it would be dark. David's apprehension grew exponentially with the descending, growing darkness. No, it wasn't dark. It was pitch black! He had thought about his nighttime experience off and on all day. In his mind, he had decided that fear was the component being measured. His reactions were of considerable scientific interest. David decided he was not going to react. He was smarter than Dr. Meddleton. He, David Carter, would show him! It would be appropriate to be the aberration or outlier in Meddleton's results. David needed to keep his reason for participating in this procedure at the front of his mind. Kay was the reason. He was going to buy her The Ring. David had moved his sleeping bag and the cot earlier in the afternoon. He had studied the diameter of the pod and had run his hands over every inch of the floor. He believed that if he stayed in the vicinity of the floor level cooler or dumbwaiter everything would be fine. He would get through this night on his terms, not Dr. Meddleton's.

Max had not paid too much attention to David for the last couple of hours. The sensors seemed to be relatively inactive but Max knew David was there and he was doing just fine. The graphs, however, should be showing more peaks. "What the hell is going on?" He started to track his graphed results. Hell, he wasn't on the cot! Where was he? Max began a methodical search of the sensors built into the pod. David was in there but according to his readings he had to be in the vicinity of the food cooler or the dumbwaiter. Well, he would fix that. Max believed that David would be getting very thirsty soon. He'd be opening the cooler to get a drink. Max had soaked some gelatinous beads earlier in the day. Their shape became deformed and enlarged with soaking. He opened the cooler from beneath. The gelatinous mass was placed in the cooler. The bottled drinks were laid on the mass. The only bottle left upright was the vitamin drink that was identified by its distinctive shape. David would have to look for his next drink. Wouldn't he be surprised! Max pushed the sliding panel on the cooler shut and sat down at his desk to await the results.

Max was thinking of the date he had arranged for Monday's lunch. His latest manoeuvre on the road to a successful conquest of Mount Helen. He enjoyed this new tactic of his. Planning out his moves as if he were going to tackle a strenuous climb. He sat back in his chair, waiting for David to get thirsty. He would need to make sure that all traces of the gelatinous mass was removed before the technicians arrived in the morning. Kay was beginning to concern him. He contemplated letting her go. Her questions and observations were becoming too frequent. If she began raising her concerns with any of his colleagues he knew there would be trouble. He would decide what to do when this session was over. Maybe he would make an appointment with Kay to discuss her future goals and her continued employment. He was also meeting with several of his colleagues later in the week. He wondered if he could get them to be part of the daytime activities of the study. That might silence his critics. He knew the gossip that was circulating. It was the result of the money. It was always the money! He had access to a "cash cow" that no one at the college had ever thought to access. "Well, that was just too damn bad." Actually, his contact with the Department of Defence (Canada) and the Americans was the result of cocktail room chitchat at a conference he had attended. The Americans wanted to be able to measure fear. They wanted to know when, if, and how to "break" a prisoner without leaving a mark on their person. There could be no physical evidence, no evidence of wrongdoing. It took a lot of effort on his part to "cloak" the research. So far, everything was working out just fine. Not a single soul at the College knew where the money actually originated! Max wanted it kept that way.

Night 3

Dr. Meddleton had a surprise for David. Tonight was the night of the noises. He had taped rats scratching and scurrying about. He had their terrified squeaks on tape when a snake was placed in the cage with them. Then, there was nothing but absolute silence until the snake found them. He had other good sounds for David Carter as well. He thought his best was the sound of dripping water, rushing water, water slapping at the sides of an object. These sounds interspersed with the rat squeaks would make for a very interesting third night for David Carter. Max did not believe that David would make it past the fourth night, if he made it past tonight, the third night. David did not.

CHAPTER 10

The End of the Black

People avoided him now. He knew it was because he stunk. David had not changed his clothes for several weeks. He had not been back to his dorm at all. He had seen Kay several times but she had not seen him. She was still searching for him. He missed her desperately. He missed her quiet company, her chuckle when something amused her, the comfort of her arms, and her magic fingers that could chase away his headaches. But it wasn't just the headaches anymore, it was the nightmares. He dared not close his eyes. He had discovered that if he did not sleep, if he wasn't in the dark, then the demons could not advance on him. David had no idea where the demons came from. He just knew they had been in the pod with him and they made themselves known in the pitch black of the room. They were even out here, out in the open. He was forever looking for light of any kind as the night began to descend. Light was the only thing keeping the demons at bay. He tried staying awake for as long as possible. That had worked for a short time but then the demons took over the dark and came alive, taking over his mind, destroying his feeble attempts at sleep or keeping them at bay. He could not take it any longer. He did not know how he had come to this state. Dirty and grungy, hair unkempt, unshaven and scraggly beard, smelling like garbage. When he saw his reflection in a window glass or mirror, he no longer recognized the reflection as himself.

He continued walking up Fortune Street. Up ahead was the new bridge. The sides were quite high, he had noticed before. The cars were whizzing past, only the engine noise giving away their size. Deep and gravelly trucks or the smooth rumble that signaled a car. When the traffic was forced to slow and then stop for a red light, none of the drivers made eye contact with him. Everyone looked the other way or looked right through him. No one saw him. All he needed was one voice, one person to take him by the hand and lead him to wherever it was light. It had to be light! He could no longer abide the dark, the voices, the moving shadows, the fingers that grew in the dark, their bony protuberances growing larger and longer to capture and devour him. David had to keep moving. Find the light, any light! The twenty-four hour establishments were few and far between. Most were restaurants or gas stations. He had been barred from nearly all the restaurants. The gas stations were not cooperative because he did not drive up in a car. Sometimes, he found a yard or a garage that had left an outside light on all night until the sun had risen. Often, he would have to move because the property owner got angry and then he would have to run until he found another source of light. If he hung around all night gas stations, the staff always called the police and then he would have to hurry away to find another source of light.

Suddenly, the lights on the bridge were extinguished. There were no cars. They were gone. There were no lights not even from any trucks. There were no trucks. The bridge was empty except for him. He had to find some light! His feet scraped the concrete of the side of the bridge. David peered over the edge. Yes, there! The light! He had to reach it.

The power failure that caused all the lights to go out made the night not just dark but black. Leaving only moonlight, which was sporadic due to the cloud cover. Then the moon appeared from behind a bank of clouds. David saw the reflection of the moonlight in the water below. He climbed up and for a moment he stood completely still on top of the railing. That one moment where he saw the moon reflected in the water below. He threw himself off the bridge and to the light. There were no screams. No cries. Just David, flying into the light, the moonlight reflected in the water. David did not have to worry about his demons ever again. He was flying into the light. Then it was black.

CHAPTER 11

The Investigation into the Untimely Death
of Dr. Maxwell Meddleton

Present Day

Bill Jessiman reported to Detective Jimmy Moore of the Murder and Violent Crimes Squad in the morning. He could not believe how excited he was. He felt like a kid at the circus! Bill had decided to take a chance and he had worn his civilian clothing. His uniform was hanging in his locker just in case he had to change.

Jimmy Moore saw Jessiman waiting in the squad room. "Hey, Jessiman, glad you're here. I want you to come with me. We are going to set up a couple of rooms in the Psych Department of River College. Once we get our appointments set up, we can start interviewing witnesses. I'm also going to need a hand with logging the audio tapes and film canister tapes. We'll need to match the tapes and filmed sessions to real people. And, in case you did not know, we have no idea who the real people are! That's our challenge. We have to be able to identify these people because maybe one of them had something to do with the murder of Dr. Meddleton. So, the fun begins. You have no idea of the road blocks the college is throwing my way. Academic freedom, privacy rights of individuals, restricted access to research notes, and on and on and on! You want to know what I think, Jessiman?" Jimmy did not wait for an answer. "If, and it's a big if, we can even pinpoint a suspect we are going to be damn lucky. It is going to take days to wade through those tapes and filmed sequences. The college won't allow them to be removed from the lab. The technicians and/or students assistants have to sign the tapes out to us. I'm about ready to cut my throat! When I heard that you used to teach, well it was like hearing the Hallelujah Chorus! You are going to be my savior, my staff, maybe even my angel of mercy or whatever I want you to be. Let me tell you, there is no way we could have dreamed up the shit Dr. Meddleton was shovelling. You would think that there would have been rules and regulations and someone keeping an eye on things. Instead, it's just a fuckin' free for all. As long as the money keeps coming in on a regular basis who cares what is going on!" Moore was wound up and he was still going strong. "I know we are going to need cases of folders because each interview will require its own folder with the following information: time and date of interview, full name and address and telephone number where we can be guaranteed to reach them, a work number if they have one and where they've been for the last forty-eight hours. The coroner has given us a time frame. It's not really exact. He's been dead a few days before he was found. But for now, we're looking at forty-eight hours but you have to know that the time frame may change. Also, their connection to Dr.

Meddleton—co-worker, student, whatever. We are going to go through his address book here and at his apartment. I have a couple of guys going through the apartment as we speak. Anything that looks like it is remotely connected to this business will be tagged and bagged and brought to the station. You are going to be working overtime, my man."

Bill Jessiman was writing everything down in his notebook as fast as he could. He hoped he had not missed anything. He would go over the details of the instructions in the car with Detective Moore. They both left the central office and headed for the parking garage. Moore waited for Jessiman to get settled in the passenger seat. He was pleased that he did not need to remind him to fasten his lap belt. He started the car, pressed his foot on the accelerator and they were on their way to River College.

Jessiman cleared his throat. "Detective Moore..."

"Listen, Jessiman, when we are on our own you can call me Jimmy. What is your first name?"

"Bill," Jessiman replied.

"Okay, I'll call you Bill when we are by ourselves and Constable Jessiman if anyone else is around. So, Bill, what do you want to know?"

"I would like to review your instructions. I want to make sure I haven't missed anything."

"No problem, go right ahead." Jimmy replied as he slowed down and stopped for a red traffic signal.

Bill Jessiman went over all the instructions he had managed to record.

Jimmy smiled and said, "The only part you've missed out on was the Hallelujah Chorus and the angel part! Just kidding. Believe me, your addition to the team was very carefully thought out. You are going to talk to these guys as if you are one of them. You know being in the vicinity of such brilliance as displayed by the River College academics makes me really nervous. These people don't know how to speak plain English. I feel like everything they say has a second meaning and they don't have time to descend to my level of understanding! Don't worry, Bill. As far as I'm concerned you will be worth your weight in gold."

Silence reigned in the car and in no time they arrived at River College. Moore parked in the first guest space and made sure the police identification was visible. They entered through the huge brass and oak doors and were headed for the dean's office when an older woman approached them.

"Detective Moore?"

"That's me," Jimmy replied.

"I'm Mrs. Poitson, the dean's administrative assistant. I'm afraid he has had to postpone his meeting with you. He's taking a very important telephone call. He will be rescheduling his appointment with you for later today."

"Thank you, Mrs. Poitson. Can you show us the rooms where we'll be working while we are on campus? But first I want to introduce Constable Jessiman. He's one of you. Now, no one will be able to bamboozle me any longer."

Mrs. Poitson smiled and shook her head. "It's nice to make your acquaintance, Constable Jessiman. Really, Detective Moore, I must take exception to your comments. No one is trying to bamboozle you! You just seem to be experiencing difficulty understanding the research ethic. Never mind, it will all come together over time. Here we are." She indicated an open doorway and motioned them both to go in ahead of her. "I have taken the liberty of making several appointments for you. I'm sure you will want to arrange the remaining appointments yourself. But I do know the schedules and availability of the staff and students and I've tried the slot the appointments with you during their free periods. I hope you don't mind?"

"No, Mrs. Poitson. I appreciate it very much because it means we can get to work immediately. Constable Jessiman will arrange the remaining appointments that we feel are necessary."

"Well, Detective Moore, I tried to make sure you would have all that you would require." She indicated the room and waved towards the adjoining room. "Each room has a desk, filing cabinet, several chairs, and a telephone that is separate from our switchboard. I've also taken the liberty of putting out some stationery supplies that you might need."

"Thank you, Mrs. Poitson. If we need anything else Constable Jessiman will contact you. By the way, do the filing cabinets and desks lock?"

Mrs. Poitson sighed. "The filing cabinets do but the desks do not."

"Don't worry, Mrs. Poitson, Constable Jessiman will get one of our technicians from the station to install locks on the desks. You've gone to a lot of trouble for us and we do appreciate it. We can take it from here."

Mrs. Poitson inquired, "Don't you want to know the times of your appointments?"

Moore smiled. "Yes, by all means. Who are we seeing and at what time?"

"At 11 am you will see Kay Osbourn, Dr. Meddleton's senior technician. At 1:30 pm it will be Janice Cameron, his other technician. At 3 pm it will be student assistant Beverly Scott. I've also taken the liberty of supplying you the timetables of anyone associated with the Sensory Deprivation Laboratory so you can arrange your appointments as conveniently as possible. We would really appreciate it if they did not miss any classes or lab sessions. They will be under even more pressure with exams just around the corner and now this business." Mrs. Poitson frowned. "I'll leave you now. I will be in my office for most of the day if you need anything else." Mrs. Poitson turned and left the room.

Detective Moore stood to one side. "Well, Jessiman, what do you think? Is there such an animal as a 'research ethic'?"

"Sir, I can't say at this time but word is trickling down about some audio tapes. They do not sound at all pleasant. If half of what I've heard is true then River College has a really big problem, research ethic or not."

Jimmy walked into the next room. He hung his jacket on the back of the chair. "Well, Bill, first things first. Get hold of a technician from the station. I want locks for the desks and replacement locks with corresponding keys for the filing cabinets and for the doors. I want to be sure that we are the only ones with access to this area. We will have the only keys. We have about an hour and a half before our first appointment arrives. Let's plan our strategy." Jimmy consulted his notes. "Kay OsbournOsbourn is the person who unlocked the lab office for the students on the Tuesday that Meddleton's body was discovered. She is Meddleton's senior technician. I'll conduct this interview but you are to listen and take notes. When I'm done, I'll ask you if you have any questions. That's when you focus on your intuition, your gut feelings, whatever. I want you to vocalize what you are thinking. If I've missed a question, you go ahead and ask. My nose won't be out of joint! If the killer is part of this research group I want him to think I'm really out to lunch. Then maybe he'll make a mistake. That's when we will go for the throat. Got it?"

"Yes, sir, Jessiman replied.

"Forget the sir when we are alone, Bill. I'm just Jimmy. I want you to hear this. I think you had better close the door." Jimmy opened his briefcase and removed a tape recorder. He slid a tape onto the spindle and pressed the play button. At first there was silence. Then a blood-curdling scream followed by rapid breath sounds, some scuffling noises that went on for several minutes and then more silence. Then the animal, or whatever it was, gave a frantic "wheep" and then silence again. The next thing Bill heard was the sound of dripping water which quickly changed to a torrent and then silence and more scuffling. Bill wiped his forehead. He was perspiring but he felt absolutely cold. "You see Bill, this is the audio tape that was on Meddleton's desk when he was found. As soon as I track down the film record... " Jimmy paused. "Once both are matched up I believe we will certainly learn more and we will know more than we ever wanted to know. In the meantime, no one knows we have this one so let's keep it that way." He turned the tape recorder off and put it back in his briefcase. "Our first interview should arrive any minute."

He had no sooner said this when there was a soft knock at the door. Bill walked over to the door and opened it. "Can I help you?"

CHAPTER 12

River College

"Hi, I'm Kay Osbourn. I'm your 11 am appointment."

Bill stepped back. "Come in Miss Osbourn." Bill turned back into the room. "Detective Moore, Miss Osbourn is here."

Jimmy walked into the room. "Miss Osbourn, glad you could make it. Have a seat." Kay sat down but she was perched on the edge of her chair. She was annoyed with Mrs. Poitson for making her the first appointment. Well, she wasn't going to let them know. Jimmy fiddled with the note pad and his pen. He and Bill exchanged a look but no words passed between them. Then Detective Moore cleared his throat and his questions began in a rapid-fire sequence and Kay felt that she had no time to think of her answers. This was not good at all. She slowed his pace somewhat with her reply to his question about the phone.

"We all share it. All seventy-two of us. The number is EDDA 3135."

"Where do you work?"

"I work in the Psychology Department here at River College."

Jimmy sighed. The first bump in the long road ahead. "Could you elaborate on that statement."

"I'm one of Dr. Meddleton's technicians. There are two of us but I'm the senior person."

"I want to know where you were for the forty-eight hours prior to the time that Dr. Meddleton's body was discovered."

Kay sat up. "I went to class, studied in the library, went to class, had supper, went to bed, got up, had breakfast, and went to class. Then it was lunchtime. I was on my way back to the dorm when one of the students found me and informed me that they were unable to get into the laboratory. I went back with him and unlocked the door and let the students in. I had already started back to the dorm when I heard the screaming. I ran back and went in and...saw him...saw Dr. Meddleton..." Kay experienced some difficulty with her narrative for several minutes. Then she continued. "Everyone was screaming. He looked dead. I knew he was dead. It was obvious." Kay stopped and took a deep breath.

"Well, Kay, that is the last twenty-four hours, now, what about the twenty-four hours previous to that?" Detective Moore asked her.

"It's pretty much the same except after classes in the afternoon and after supper I got my car and went for a drive."

"By yourself?" Detective Moore asked.

"Yes," Kay said. "I needed to think and I usually drive out towards the countryside, somewhere without people around so I can think my problems through without interruptions."

"Problems? A pretty girl like you has problems?"

Kay's head jerked upwards involuntarily. "Yes, Detective, I've got problems."

"Would these problems have anything to do with Dr. Meddleton?"

Kay sighed. "In a way. I've been thinking about quitting as his technician."

"Why?" asked Detective Moore.

"My job was more like a supervisor. I made sure meals were placed in the dumb waiter on time and changes of clothing as required would also be taken care of by the technicians on duty. It was very important that there was no delay in providing the meals or the changes of clothing. The experience needed to as stressless as possible. For session one, that wasn't a problem. If the subjects decided to quit they had a panic button to use. My duties involved watching the films from the daytime sessions of session one. I catalogued everything they did while in the pod. Janice, the other technician, discussed a concern she had regarding one of the subjects. She did not want Dr. Meddleton to know I had seen a tape from the second session, or that we had discussed anything about the subjects. Dr. Meddleton is very...was very strict about that. Dr. Meddleton had invited me to view a film from the second session. It wasn't the same one that Janice showed me but it was just as bad. I did not like what I saw. It made me very uncomfortable. He, that is Dr. Meddleton, told me he would let me listen to an audio session from the nighttime second sessions when he felt I was ready."

Detective Moore sat back. "We're almost done here. What do you think Constable Jessiman?"

Bill looked down at his notebook. "If you don't mind, Miss Osbourn, I have one or two questions. Do you live at the residence year-round?"

"No, I go home and stay with my folks."

"Where is home?"

"Carberry, the other side of Brandon. We have a farm, a cattle farm."

"What do you do at home? Do you help with the work?"

"Yes, I help with the milking and at harvest I help my dad with the combining and baling and I also help my mom with the cooking."

"Sounds like a really good life."

"Yes, it is. I love it."

"When you went on your drive before and after supper did you see anyone you know? Do you know if anyone saw you? Maybe you can remember some of your route?"

Kay thought for a moment. "No, I never saw anyone at all. As for where I drove, I know I drove southeast of the college onto the highway and I really don't remember much except coming back. It was very late and I was very tired."

"Why didn't you approve of the film that Dr. Meddleton previewed for you?" Bill asked. His voice adjusted so that he sounded more curious than questioning.

"You have to understand, for the first session the people or subjects can be in total darkness or total light for at least five days and five nights. Or, they can be in complete daylight with no night because that feature can be controlled. They undergo several tests before and after and during their time in the pod. They also have access to a panic button that they can use at any time during the session. The film I saw from the second session was done in the daytime. I never saw anything like it, ever." Kay stated quite emphatically.

"Did he play the audio tapes for you?"

"No, but the tape I did preview was a woman and you could tell by her behaviour that she was close to cracking up."

"What do you mean "cracking up,"" Jessiman asked.

"She looked like she was near to having a nervous breakdown. She had facial twitches. She was picking at her arms, hard enough to cause minor bleeds. She was very, very jumpy. I asked Dr. Meddleton how far into the sessions she got before she used the panic button. He said she did not use the panic button at all. Then, just as I was leaving, he told me there wasn't a panic button for the second session participants! It wasn't right!"

Jessiman thought for a moment. "Do you have any idea who this woman might have been?"

Kay paused before answering. "No. The film was identified by SQ61. But I remember Dr. Meddleton calling her Sheila and remarking that she was not as brave as she thought she was. The way he said Sheila, it wasn't a compliment. He had total disdain in his voice. It was like he couldn't wait to be rid of her."

"One last question, Miss Osbourn. Someone must know who these people were who went through the second session. Where are those records kept?"

"I don't know. I don't know." Suddenly Kay put her

hands over her face, her shoulders shaking. "I'm sorry, please may I go?" Kay looked at them both. The tears were coursing down her cheeks. Bill looked over at Jimmy.

Jimmy shrugged and said, "If you've no more questions, Constable Jessiman, I think were done for now. We will be in touch again in the next few days, although it may take up to ten days before we get back to you, Miss Osbourn. If you decide to take a trip home, please let us know. I appreciate your cooperation in this very difficult situation."

Kay stood and wiped at her face with her sleeve. Jessiman walked her to the door and closed it behind her.

CHAPTER 13

Bill turned to Jimmy but Detective Moore held up his hand.

"No, Bill, no discussions, yet. We'll make our notes and put the file away. If other questions come to mind, jot them down for the next sessions we will have with her. There will be several next sessions, you can be sure of that. We'll discuss everyone's stories after we're done with them. For now, we are done here. I'm going to write up my thoughts and impressions and I suggest that you do the same. By the time we're done with this our next interview should be knocking on the door."

Jimmy turned and went into his adjoining room. Bill Jessiman went over to his desk. He prepared a double set of folders for all the interviews—one set for him and one set for Detective Moore. These interviews were going to keep them tied up for the next several days, perhaps even longer. Bill walked into Jimmy's office and put them on his desk. He returned to his room and went over his notes. The answers to all the questions and the reactions elicited were noted as well. He sat there thinking, staring into space, then made several more notations in the margin (right-handed or left-handed, estimated weight of assailant, remember to ask her again where she drove, the miles covered according to her mileage indicator). Maybe with luck she might remember something else. Bill put his notes into the folder. Then he got his notebook out. He had a new one for this assignment. He entered a shortened version of the interview and his margin notes, along with his impression of Kay Osbourn (angry, petulant, defensive, feels guilty—why, and his final thought–who is Kay Osbourn? Who is the person behind that face?) He filed the folder away behind the interview divider.

Bill remembered that he had to phone the station and request the services of a technician. He got through to Physical Resources rather quickly he thought. The technician promised to pick up the locks and be there to install them around three-thirty in the afternoon. Bill had just put the phone down when there was a knock at the door. He got up to answer it. "Yes, can I help you?"

The gentleman standing in the doorway was of medium height and portly. He had rosy-hued cheeks and silver hair. "Dean Sullivan, Detective Moore."

"Sorry, Dean Sullivan, I'm Constable Jessiman. Just a moment. I'll get Detective Moore for you." Bill knocked on the connecting door that Jimmy had closed.

"Yes, Bill? What is it?"

Bill opened the door. "Dean Sullivan is here to see you."

"How long till our next appointment?" Jimmy asked him.

"About ten minutes."

"Fine, tell Dean Sullivan I'll be right out."

Bill stepped back and trod on the Italian leather clad toes of Dean Sullivan. "Excuse me, Dean Sullivan. Detective Moore will be with you in a moment." Bill reached forward and pulled the connecting door closed.

Dean Sullivan rubbed his hands together while exclaiming under his breath, "Dear me, there is a problem. I must speak with Detective Moore at once. This cannot wait."

The door opened and Jimmy walked out. He greeted Dean Sullivan and shook hands with him. "I couldn't help but hear what you were saying Dean Sullivan. What cannot wait? Why don't we walk out to the lobby. It is kind of dark in here and Constable Jessiman has another interview beginning in a few minutes. Jessiman, you can go ahead with the interview. Same routine as earlier. I'll ask my questions when I return. I won't be long." He paused for a moment "And, Jessiman, make sure you leave the door partially open, okay?" Bill nodded.

Detective Moore and Dean Sullivan walked across the rotunda. "Let's sit here, Dean Sullivan. Now, why not tell me what the problem is."

Dean Sullivan spoke quickly and sounded totally overwhelmed. "I just got off the telephone with some naval people. Americans from the States. They got my number from Ottawa! They are coming here! They want access to Meddleton's lab and files! What was he doing? Department of Defense...the naval people...I don't know what to think."

"Did they say when they would be arriving?"

"No, not really, except that they are on their way. They were catching a 2:00 pm flight out of Bethesda and then connecting with a regular carrier service. Probably Air Canada. They will probably arrive sometime tomorrow."

Jimmy took a deep breath. "Don't do anything, Dean Sullivan. Just leave it all to me. I appreciate the heads up. I'll take it from here. I know you have a lot on your plate right now and I'll get Mrs. Poitson to give me an appointment to see you later this week." He paused. "That's if it is okay with you?"

"Yes of course, very kind of you, young man." Dean Sullivan stood up and headed back to his office. Jimmy looked around and saw a bank of payphones on the far side by the floor to ceiling windows. He strode over, put in the required change, and dialed the chief's number. He answered on the third ring. "Chief. Moore here. I've got a big problem." He explained the details and then went on. "I am going to need three or four really big guys from the station that can't be intimidated by anyone to guard Dr. Meddleton's research space. Also, can you give me a couple of clerks, lots of boxes. I am going to have the lab contents removed either to our workspace or to the station. I haven't decided where for sure yet. Can we get a judge to cover what we are doing?"

The chief cleared his throat. "Do you believe the lab contents are vital to this investigation?"

"Yes, Chief, I do. I'm basing this on the single tape that I lifted from Meddleton's desk. I've left Jessiman to question the next witness. I'm going back there right away. As soon as the men get here and the clerks arrive, I'll put them to work. The sooner they can get here the better. Also, I interviewed one of his technicians and she voiced serious concerns about the research Meddleton was carrying out."

"I'll get you what you want right away. Everything you need should be there within an hour or two. I'll have to get a judge to sign off on this but I think I know who to get in touch with. As soon as I have the warrant it will be delivered to you. It is possible that the judge may want to speak with you beforehand."

"Thanks, Chief. I'll be in touch." Jimmy ended the call and headed back to the temporary office space. He stood outside for a few minutes listening to Jessiman questioning Janice Cameron, Meddleton's other technician. He knocked softly on the door before he entered. Bill looked up, "I'm done here. Detective Moore, this is Janice Cameron."

"Hi, Janice. I do have some questions for you but right now I have a bit of an emergency on my hands. I'm going to need you to unlock Dr. Meddleton's research area for me. I just finished talking to Dean Sullivan, so let's head up there." Jimmy had no qualms about letting Janice Cameron think the dean had approved the unlocking of Meddleton's research rooms. "Bill, you can meet us up there. Be sure to lock up here." Jimmy held the door open for Janice and hustled her along the corridor to the elevator. Janice could hardly keep up with him.

"Detective Moore, I have a class in fifteen minutes."

"Not to worry, Janice, Dean Sullivan is meeting me up there. Just unlock the door and get to your class. If you like, you can give me your key. I can return it to the dean and you can pick it up from him or Mrs. Poitson."

"My classes go until seven-thirty tonight. I won't be

able to get the key back until after lunch tomorrow. Actually, if anyone needs me they can let the dean's office know. I don't want the key!"

"I'll be sure to let the dean and/or Mrs. Poitson know. Don't worry." Janice unlocked the doors to the observation room, the testing pod, and Max Meddleton's office. "Janice, can I ask you a question?"

"Sure."

"Didn't the people who took part know this door was here?"

"No, Detective Moore. On the other side, it just looks like the wall. The research subjects always entered the pod from the trapdoor entrance. The darkness they were subjected to always disoriented them quite a bit."

"Right, I forgot about that."

"Is there anything else?" Janice asked.

Jimmy held out his hand. "Just the key, Janice."

"Oh, I forgot. Here it is." She took the key off of her key ring and handed it to Detective Moore.

"If you don't mind, Janice. One more question. What was your opinion of the research being carried on here?"

"Well, I thought it was okay, except for the audio tape I previewed a couple of days ago." Janice paused as if thinking about how much she should say.

"Go on." Detective Moore encouraged her with a smile.

"Well, the subject, it was a man. His reactions were totally different from the others. He acted really scared, even terrified, and that was almost from the very beginning. I could not talk to Dr. Meddleton about it because he would just get really angry. He told me before not to question what he is doing because I don't know anything! I left a message for Kay Osbourn. She and I listened to the tape together. Kay was really upset. I mean she did not say anything but I could tell from her face. She was just so pale. She said she would talk to Dr. Meddleton. May I go now, Detective Moore?"

"Sure, Janice, off you go and thanks for the key. I'll see to it that it gets back to the dean's office. Jimmy turned back into the observation room. He listened to Janice's retreating footsteps as she hurried down the hall.

CHAPTER 14

Jimmy pulled the door partially shut and then went over to Dr. Meddleton's desk. He opened the drawers and began removing everything to the tabletop to the left of the desktop. He was grateful that the crime scene cleanup crew had already been in and done their job. He could make use of the desktop. He could still picture the crime scene in his head. As he emptied the drawers each pile was identified as to its original location—drawer one, long middle drawer, drawer two, etc. He removed the folders, stacking them on the floor. Each set of stacks again was labelled according to the drawer it was from. While he stacked the folders, he opened several at random. He noted the research had been going on for at least three years. He wondered where Dr. Meddleton kept the information that had Janice and Kay so concerned.

Jimmy began pulling books off of the shelves. They too were stacked on the floor and labeled as to their orientation—shelf one, window, etc. He came across some very large binder-type reference books. The spine of each binder was labelled *Bethesda*. He opened one of them. There were about twenty-five dividers in each and each section held several envelopes in individual holders. He opened one up. There was a typed transcript of the audio tape and a film canister. Jimmy had found the Session Two material! He was elated. Just then, there was a light knock on the door. He turned around. Bill Jessiman entered and right behind him were the four burly officers. Everyone was carrying a stack of folding boxes.

"The clerks are following with more boxes," Bill told Jimmy. "What's happening?"

Jimmy sighed and then explained. "Well, it is like this. Some U.S. Navy research people are arriving either late tonight or early tomorrow. They want to restrict access to the lab and to the files. We need to get everything out of here and placed somewhere secure." He paused for a moment. "For sure not here. Somewhere at the station. Once the interviews are done we'll be doing most of our work at the station. You know that old saying about 'possession being nine points of the law'. Well, that's going to be us for a change. We are going to have possession. Once we are done with the investigation, the Bethesda people can have the whole shooting match. In fact, they can fight it out with Dean Sullivan and River College over who will have possession of the files. But right now there's no way any of this is leaving the city or this province before I say we're done with it. Our last interview today should be at our temporary office. We'll do it in stages like we did with the Cameron girl. I'll see how we're doing here. I want this all outta here no later than eight tonight. I'll arrange for a truck for 7:30 pm. We'll get it all loaded and be back at the station before anyone knows what we are up to. Once the clerks start their work here, lock the door. I do not want anyone walking in unexpectedly and raising a ruckus. Constable Jessiman and I will be back as soon as possible. By the way, those four binders labelled Bethesda? Pack them up separately. We will take them back with us when we leave. I'll arrange for the truck and I am going to check on the status of the warrant with the chief. Okay, Jessiman, let's get back to our little cubbyhole. Beverly Scott should be arriving any minute. I want to go over your impressions of the interviews with Janice Cameron and Kay Osbourn. I don't know how much longer Dr. Meddleton could have kept this going if Janice Cameron's comments are anything to go by. Whatever he was doing was sure making her uneasy. Did you know she contacted Kay Osbourn about one of the audio tapes? I sure would like to talk to whomever is on that tape." Moore and Jessiman were back at the College assigned rooms. Approaching them from the other side of the building was a petite, beautiful, drop-dead gorgeous girl. Moore addressed her.

"Miss Scott?" She nodded her assent. "I'm Detective Moore and this is Constable Jessiman." He pointed to Bill who was unlocking the door. Bill nodded.

"You are our last appointment this afternoon. We'll be setting up the other appointments for later tomorrow afternoon and the day after if need be. Come on in."

Beverly hesitated on the threshold. "I don't know why I have to talk to you. I don't know anything. I wasn't even here when they found Max. I mean…Dr. Meddleton." Beverly looked like she was going to burst into tears. Detective Moore smiled and put out his hand to comfort her.

"It's okay, Beverly. The appointments were set up by Mrs. Poitson. Any students who had contact outside of class time with Dr. Meddleton and who had a free period today. An appointment has been set up. That way no one misses out on their other classes or any other labs. You know, we only have a few questions. Just relax. Don't worry. Jessiman and I are both going to sit down with you and we both may even have some questions for you. Just answer as best and as truthfully as you can."

Detective Moore indicated a chair for Beverly to sit on. He went behind the desk and Jessiman moved his chair so that he could watch Beverly without being in her face. The questioning began and continued in an uneventful fashion until Jessiman asked "What was your relationship to Dr. Meddleton?"

Beverly blushed a bright scarlet and then looked down at the floor.

"Miss Scott?" Jimmy reminded Beverly that they were waiting for her answer.

Beverly still looked down at the floor. She appeared to be examining the flooring very carefully. Then, so softly that they had to strain to hear what she said, "We were not seeing each other anymore." Beverly looked up and in a stronger voice she stated, "I dropped him."

"You were dating?" Jessiman asked.

"Yes."

Detective Moore inquired, "Is it allowed for an instructor to date his or her student?"

Again, Beverly's voice dropped significantly. "No. You won't tell anyone, will you?"

"I can't promise anything on that score, Beverly." Jimmy advised her. Then he asked, "Were you having a sexual relationship or a platonic one?"

Beverly gave a small secret smile and replied, "It wasn't platonic at all." Then the questions came at her in rapid fire sequence. She had no time to think about what she was saying to Moore or Jessiman.

"When was the last time you saw Dr. Meddleton?"

"About a month ago."

"You haven't seen him since?"

"No."

"What about your classes or the labs? Did you have any contact then?" Jessiman asked her.

"Not unless I had a question or theory that needed explaining. We were very careful in class and out of class. No one knew."

Jessiman looked at her. "No one knew about what?"

"That we were seeing one another. That we were dating," Beverly replied. Jessiman knew she was wrong about that. Someone always knew. People talked. Jimmy took over at this point.

"When you say dating, you mean he took you out to places?"

Beverly looked somewhat put out. "Yes."

Jimmy sighed. "You know, Beverly, I find it hard to believe that no one saw you if he took you places."

"Well, of course, we were seen at different functions but we did not arrive together. We never arrived together and we never left together. No one knew we were seeing one another. I couldn't even tell my best friend. Max made me promise!"

Jimmy shook his head, "Well, time will tell, I suppose. If we need to ask you any more questions, where can you be reached if you are not staying in the residence?"

"I live at home," Beverly said.

Jimmy lifted an eyebrow. "And where might home be?"

"Woodhaven Boulevard."

"What is your telephone number at home, Beverly?" Jimmy asked.

"CRAY 2830." Suddenly Beverly looked unnerved. "You can't say anything to my parents. They will kill me! My Dad is a Deacon at our church."

Jimmy just shook his head. "Well, Miss Scott, we'll do our best to keep your secret a secret. However, it might end up coming out regardless of what we do. But you might get lucky. I cannot say right this minute how all of this will play out. I do want to thank you for your cooperation. There is one last question before you go. Where were you between 11 pm and 4 am on the day Professor Meddleton was killed?"

Beverly paled. Her eyes took on a haunted expression. She stammered "Wh- wh- where was I when Max was k-k-killed? Why? I didn't k-k-kill him!"

Jimmy reassured her as best he could. "It's a question we are asking everyone."

Beverly shifted in her chair, she crossed her ankles, concentrating on something on the floor. Her head down, her face hidden from Detective Moore and Constable Jessiman by her long hair falling forward to cover her face.

"Miss Scott? Is there a problem?"

Beverly sighed and then looked up. She shoved her hair off her face with her fingers. She looked at Detective Moore. Her eyes appeared to darken and her lips appeared compressed and thinner. "I was waiting for Max."

Both men managed to hide their surprise rather well. "You were waiting for Professor Meddleton?"

"Yes, I fell asleep waiting for him."

Jimmy paused and then asked, "Where were you waiting for him?"

Beverly sneered. "I suppose one of his nosey old lady neighbours will tell you. I was at his apartment."

Detective Moore noticed that Jessiman was looking taken aback by her response.

"Did he know you were waiting for him?"

"No, I was going to surprise him."

"Did you surprise him often?"

"No, this was only the third or fourth time. My parents were away for the weekend. They wouldn't have known anything about it. I fell asleep waiting for Max. When he didn't show up I left his key on the counter and took off. I was home by 2:30 am."

Bill Jessiman asked Beverly, "Did anyone see you leave or see you get home?"

"Well, I called a cab. I called Moore's."

"Well, Beverly, we'll check your statement out with the cab company. Hopefully the driver and dispatcher can back up your claim as to the time of departure from Meddleton's apartment and your arrival time at home."

Jimmy Moore and Jessiman both watched her as she

quickly walked away. Her hip movement with each step caused them both to glance at each other appreciatively.

CHAPTER 15

Possession and the Evidence

Jimmy cleared his throat and advised Bill that they had better check on the movers in the lab area. He would leave two of the constables guarding the locked empty room. Their instructions were that no one was allowed in without Moore's approval. The rooms were a crime scene and there would be no tampering of evidence. There was no point in the College or the Bethesda people finding out too soon that the lab had been cleaned out and was now totally empty. Jimmy knew that there was going to be trouble but he also knew he had preempted the Americans. By removing the material from the lab he had outmanoeuvred the possibility of their retention of the materials. All the books, binders, tapes, and photos would be the property of the Winnipeg Police until they were done with it all.

Jimmy and Bill took the elevator to the lab. Everything was packed up and ready to be transported by truck back to the station. Jimmy made sure that they understood nothing was to be removed until after hours. Once everything was out, the lab would be locked up and the two constables were to remain on guard until midnight. Then two more would return for their shift. They would relieve each other at five-hour intervals for at least two or three days and nights. Under no circumstances were they to let anyone into the rooms and they were not to divulge to anyone from the College that the rooms were empty, so to speak. Jimmy and Bill picked up the binders that had been packed into two boxes for them and left for the station. The drive there was completed with them both in deep in thought. Jimmy Moore was surprised when they appeared to have arrived at the station. He wondered how he had managed that. He really could not remember any portion of the drive.

Three hours later the last box had been carried to a waiting moving van. Jimmy had decided it was safe for two trainees to accompany the truck back to the station. They would meet at the loading dock and get everything into another secured room at the station. Jimmy was not sure how Bill Jessiman was going to find an extra empty room. Hell, he thought they might have to take over the chief's office! He knew there would be big-time grief very shortly. The Bethesda people should be landing soon. The guards could hold them off for a day or two but not much longer than that and then the Bethesda people and the dean would discover that Dr. Meddleton's office was empty!

Jimmy had arranged for a photographer to take pictures of the room where the Session Two work had taken place. He had also ordered pictures of Dr. Meddleton's home and pictures of anything they found that was believed to be central to their investigation including the dumbwaiter that brought food and drink to the participants. Now, it had all been secured in the lockup and the key could not be left anywhere where someone, anyone could help themselves to it. It would not be the first-time evidence had disappeared but it was not going to disappear on his watch. He and Bill needed to go somewhere quiet, with no listening walls, to discuss the case. It was this kind of discussion that made Jimmy the excellent detective he was. He did not mind sharing his thoughts and often the discussion would lead him in a direction he might not have taken. The new direction quite often resulted in really good leads and sometimes even arrests.

Jimmy helped to unload the van on the station loading ramp. Jessiman had found a room. It was off of the Conference Rooms and it had its own key. No one seemed to know what the room's purpose had been. It contained a long metal table and a couple of chairs. The ceiling lights would need to be replaced as several had already blown but at least they could go through everything up there without trucking the boxes off to another room. Everything was as secure as they could make it. In a few days they would call the men off of the empty room's detail. The Bethesda people were due to arrive in a couple of hours. Jimmy felt sorry for the dean. He had no idea how he was going to stand up to those hard cases. But he smiled as he thought how the shit would soon hit the fan. He was ready. They could raise all the ruckus they wanted. It would get them nowhere.

"Well, we're here. Let's go find the chief and see where we can find a projector and reel to reel tape recorder. I want to see some of these films and I want the chief to hear some of the audio tapes. Unless he hears them firsthand he just won't believe what we're dealing with. I'm even having trouble accepting what we're dealing with here. Bill, do you mind taking the boxes in with you? I'll go and get the chief. We'll see you shortly." Jimmy Moore ran up the stairs and into the station. Bill Jessiman picked up the two boxes of binders and carried them in. He left the boxes in the care of the Desk Sergeant and went to locate and set up their space.

They would probably need at least two other smaller rooms and they had to be able to lock them up from the inside as well as the outside. Once they began listening to the audio tapes and watching the filmed sequences there could no possibility of anyone walking in without warning. He suspected that they were dealing with some very sensitive material. He also wanted to be close to the evidence room so that the length of time between packing up and and putting everything away was as short as possible. In the end, Jessiman opted for a larger room on the first floor by the back stairwell. The entry to the evidence room was just to the right of these stairs. He got the room ready for Jimmy and the chief. He had located a tape recorder that would play reel to reel and he had the projector set up for the films. Finding the binders was certainly going to make their job a lot easier. He glanced over at a calendar that was on the wall. Today was Thursday. He would be seeing his sergeant after six pm. He had better make sure he was prepared. While he was waiting for Jimmy, he took his notebook out of his pocket. He reviewed his entries. He updated the final interview with Beverly Scott and made a note of Jimmy's conversation with the dean about the arrival of the Bethesda Naval investigators. Bill had just tucked his notebook away when Jimmy walked in with the chief.

"Constable Jessiman." The chief acknowledged him with a nod of his head.

"Are we ready to roll, Bill?" Jimmy Moore asked.

"Yes, let me start the projector for you. I don't think you want to listen to the tapes along with the films do you?"

"No, listening separately from watching is how we should do it. If we tried doing both together we might all get physically sick." Bill Jessiman turned out the lights. He left one on, just so that they wouldn't be completely in the dark. "Which film are we watching?"

Bill replied, "I thought I'd start with the binder that seems to be the most recent. It would appear that each binder contains a specific number of envelopes and each envelope has a matching audio tape and film canister. This film is around the middle of the binder. It's identified by the SQ50 designation."

They sat in silence. Other than their breathing and the whirring of the projector motor there was no other noise in the room. Finally, it was over. A heavy, oppressive silence filled the room.

The chief was the first to speak. "My God, I cannot believe what I've just seen. This is not research. It is torture. I don't want to listen to an audio tape yet. Put another film on."

Jessiman rewound the film and put it the back in its envelope. He flipped the paged envelopes of the binder and finally settled on SQ62. The three men were mesmerized. Unexpectedly, Jessiman halted the film for a moment.

"Do you know who this is?" he asked them.

Jimmy shook his head. The chief looked questioningly at Jessiman. "Should I know this person?"

Jessiman's voice shook. "It's Sheila. Tony Pritchard's wife."

The chief wiped his forehead. He didn't know it but the perspiration was beading up and running down his face to his neck. "What are we going to do?" he asked before his voice cracked.

Jimmy Moore was pacing the room. "Chief, we are going to need some professional advice on this. No offense intended, but I think this has just evolved into something bigger than us, bigger than your office, and way bigger than we thought it would ever be. Let's finish watching the film. Then, we'll listen to the audio tape that matches. I think listening to one audio tape today will be enough. I have a friend who heads up Psychiatry at the Grace Hospital. Maybe I can get his help here. What do you think?"

The chief hesitated for a moment. "We'll listen to the audio tape that goes with this film. I don't want to listen to the tape for the other film we've seen. This friend of yours better be more than a GP with an interest in psychiatry and for sure not a psychologist. That's what Dr. Meddleton was. If your friend wants to consult with someone he can but the fewer people who are in the know the better off we'll be.

"No problem, Chief. My guy is in charge of the Psychiatric Ward at the Grace Hospital. The Grace may not have the prestige of the St. Boniface or General Hospitals but their Psychiatric Ward has had excellent on-site visits from the experts."

"Fine, let's get this over with." Jessiman set the projector going to finish off the film.

At one point, Jimmy Moore walked over to the light switches and turned them all on. The temperature of the room rose accordingly but they did not care. Once it was done Jimmy and the chief just sat there saying nothing. Jessiman put the audio tape into the reel-to-reel tape recorder but he did not start the machine up. Finally, Jimmy Moore reached over and flicked the switch.

"Let's get this over with. When I get home, I'm going to drink myself into oblivion." It did not matter that they knew what was happening, or they thought they knew what was happening as they listened to the audio tape that corresponded to Sheila Pritchard's film. Finally, the audio portion of the tape finished. Jimmy leaned over and switched it to rewind. No one spoke for several minutes.

Then the chief spoke up. "No one, and I mean no one, is to say anything about this to Pritchard. You cannot talk amongst yourselves and you cannot tell your wives about this. The last thing we need is Pritchard going off the deep end. Hopefully, what we've found here will help the medical people help Sheila Pritchard but no one is to say a word to anyone until we've discussed it with the psychiatrist from the Grace Hospital. Jimmy, when the truck gets here with the materials that you are having moved make sure the room is secure and that no one else has a key except you and Jessiman. In fact, I don't think the keys should be kept on your person. Make sure the Desk Sergeant locks them in the safe whenever you are done with them. I have a feeling that those Naval people are going to try and move heaven and earth to get these files and films. We had better make sure our precautions are iron clad. Jimmy, I'm leaving that up to you. By the way, Jessiman, it is six-thirty. Aren't you late for your appointment with the sergeant? You might not have been aware, Jimmy, but the sergeant is meeting with Jessiman every Thursday at 6 pm to discuss how his experience with you is developing and to give him some in-house coaching if you want to call it that. And Jessiman, not a word to him about Sheila Pritchard, is that clear?"

"Yes sir, Chief. I'll come back and help you clean up, Jimmy, as soon as I'm done." He excused himself and grabbed the elevator to where his sergeant was waiting for him.

"I think meeting with his training sergeant is an excellent idea, Chief. It will help him put things into perspective. This is also an opportunity for sharing and not sharing. I'm sure he'll do just fine. Bill Jessiman is going to need some time to process all this. I'm going to take him with me when we go to the Grace Hospital. He will also be there when the films are played and the audio tapes are listened to. Between the two of us and Dr. Kroeker, the psychiatrist, we'll be fine. I am going to check to see if the court order has been delivered yet. I'll see you tomorrow."

CHAPTER 16

Moore smiled to himself as he carried the binders down to the evidence room. Here he was doing grunt work. It wouldn't kill him and it was not like this was going to happen every day. He was enjoying his time with Jessiman. He didn't talk much but he listened and he learned. Jimmy felt that Jessiman had the makings of a really good detective. He smiled as he thought of the last question that Jessiman had asked Beverly Scott. That one had opened up some doors for them.

Jimmy Moore opened up the evidence room doors and went in. The box the binders were in went into another larger box. He closed the lid and put the name Scott on the box. He hoped that the name would not pique any curiosity seekers. It really wasn't a name connected to the bones of the case. He moved some boxes aside to make room for his larger box. It was dark enough in the room that no one would notice that this box did not have a lot of dust on it. He left the evidence room and signed himself out. There would be no way for anyone to know what he had been doing because other than signing himself in and out there was no one else down here. That was one way of achieving some sort of confidentiality to the whole process. Jimmy went out the heavy steel doors and upstairs to his desk where he cleaned up and then headed for home and the drinks he had promised himself.

Bill Jessiman and his sergeant had a very productive hour. Talking to the sergeant had helped Bill put the various interviews into words, and as well, to frame some additional questions he wanted to discuss with Jimmy. His sergeant agreed with Jessiman that the Scott girl wasn't a very likely suspect, all things considered. Finally, they were done for this week and Bill stood up to take his leave.

"Well, Constable Jessiman, do you want to remain on the case? If you want to pull out it's okay. This case is way more complicated than I expected it to be."

"No, Sergeant , I want to stay on. The opportunity I've been given by you and the chief is unbelievable and I would be an idiot to walk out on it. I'll learn more and get the kind of experience that is totally impossible to get unless one is in the field. Also, being able to work with Detective Moore is great. He is calm and level-headed and he is a terrific person to be learning investigative techniques from."

The sergeant nodded his agreement "That's great then. We'll leave things as they are. I'll see you next week for sure. Take care." Jessiman closed the door behind him.

He wanted to get home to his wife. He wanted to hug her and hold her tight and he could not tell her why he felt so desperate. He decided to buy her some flowers even though she would drive him crazy asking why he had brought her flowers. He felt it was the only thing he could do. He could not afford an expensive gift. Besides, a gift would make her even more suspicious. He left the station without meeting any other fellows. He had arranged for a room to hold all the stuff being removed from Meddleton's lab, office, and apartment. Tomorrow he would start unpacking and listing everything. Some things would stay in the boxes and some might end up out in the open on shelving that he had requisitioned. The cabinets he had ordered would hold the contents of the desk, the lab contents, and Dr. Meddleton's shelves at the lab and at his apartment. He was going to need some assistance, probably clerical, and he wasn't sure how that was going to be arranged. But as of now, he knew there would be no free time. He was up to his neck in this. He arrived at the parkade and used his ID card to get the gates to lift up so he could leave. He knew where he could stop off to buy some flowers. He was going to buy some long-stemmed roses for Donna. She was worth every penny that they were going to cost. He was home. He parked his car in the driveway, bent down to pick up the flowers from the front seat and walked up the sidewalk to the back door. He saw Donna standing at the sink. The kitchen window was open and some really good smells were making their way outside. He could hardly wait to see what was for supper.

She greeted him with a smile. "So how is the magnificent detective today?" He thrust the wrapped flowers at her.

"Bill, what are these for?" He took them from her and put them on the table, then he wrapped his arms around her.

"They are for you because I love you. I know I don't say it often enough but even if I don't tell you, I know I should. And often."

"Bill Jessiman, I just don't know. I love you, too. Now, let me unwrap these flowers." Donna tore away the paper wrappings very carefully. "Oh my, these are unbelievable." She feasted her eyes on the red long-stemmed roses. There were more than a dozen of them, that was for sure.

"Bill Jessiman, I'm sure glad you love me. I know I love you." She held him in her arms and they exchanged a long loving kiss. Donna finally pulled away. "I need to get my grandmother's vase. Your roses need a container that is worthy of them. I haven't used that vase since my grandmother left it to me. I will dish out your supper as soon as I'm done with the roses. You can go and wash up and change. In fact, if you want a shower there is time for that, too. I just wish I had fixed you something special for supper!"

"Well, don't worry. I could smell supper when I was coming up the walk and it smells delicious! I think I will have that shower. I'll be back down in about half an hour."

Donna watched him go upstairs. Something was going on at work. She didn't know what but whatever it was she knew he was worried. Donna went into the dining room and opened up the glass-fronted china cabinet. She very carefully withdrew a shimmering crystal vase. She carried it to the kitchen and put lukewarm water in, about three inches worth. Then she filled the sink with cold water and put the stems of the roses in the water. She got her snips out of the drawer and very carefully snipped about an inch and a half from each stem at an angle. Then each stem was placed into the vase. She stood gazing at the finished effect. Bill had brought her two dozen roses. They were magnificent! Whatever had happened at work had brought this on. She was not going to pepper him with questions. When he was able to talk about it he would. She would just make sure that home was where he could forget what was going on at work. Home was where he could relax and be himself. She knew that some of her friends hated the fact that their husbands would not discuss the job with them but she knew that the guys were not supposed to discuss on-going investigations. Confidentiality and no leaks of information were paramount. Sometimes, Bill would ask her a question. It would not seem like it had anything to do with whatever had been going on with the job but later on he might mention that her answer had been very helpful. By then she had usually forgotten what the original question had been. She was just glad that he thought she had been helpful.

She and Bill would be spending part of tomorrow afternoon with Dennis and Sheila's children. She had baked a pile of chocolate chip cookies to take with her. Cookies went a long way towards making things better. She knew better was a long way off.

CHAPTER 17

The alarm barely trilled when Bill reached up to shut it off. He rolled over and sat up. Donna murmured in her sleep. Bill yawned as he reached for his robe. He had said he would help with the dishes but he wasn't going to wake Donna. He would do the dishes and think about the case. He needed some extra thinking time. There was something he was missing. Something even Jimmy Moore may have missed as well. The shadow of the thought kept eluding him. He would almost grasp it and then it would vanish into thin air. He would wash up and let the dishes air dry. Donna would be up by the time he was finished showering. They would have breakfast together for a change. He glanced into the living room on his way into the kitchen. The roses were really outstanding and he found their scent to be very soothing.

Bill ran the water into the sink. He was soon done with all the dishes. He put coffee on and went back upstairs to shower and get ready for work. He and Jimmy were going to see the psychiatrist from the Grace Hospital today. They also had to schedule several more interviews. He wanted to interview the students that had been there when the body was discovered. He also wanted to interview some of the students in the dorm, especially if they were close to Kay. He intended to interview some of Beverly's classmates and friends. He wanted to know just how secret Beverly's meetings with Meddleton had been or, was it common knowledge and she just didn't know that.

He shaved, combed his hair, and made a mental note for himself to pick up a new toothbrush. The bristles on this one were wearing down. He needed to press much harder than before to achieve the same effect. He tightened his towel around his waist and went back into the bedroom.

He bent down to Donna. Her arms encircled his neck. "Love you."

"Love you, too," he replied. "I've got coffee on. You want to join me for breakfast?"

"Love to. Give me twenty minutes and I'll be right down. You make the toast and I'll do the eggs and tomato slices. No bacon though, Bill, okay?"

"Sure, I can live without bacon once in a while. I'd rather have it when we go out for breakfast, then it really is a treat."

Donna got out of bed, and headed for the bathroom. Bill finished dressing and went downstairs to start the toast and slice the tomatoes. In no time at all Donna was downstairs. The eggs were cracked into the pan. He had his over easy and she always had hers sunny-side up. The trouble with sunny-side up eggs in a restaurant was that few grill people or even cooks could prepare them so that they were totally cooked. More often than not the whites resembled snot. Donna invariably had to return the eggs to be done again. Mind you, this was happening less often since she had started ordering her eggs basted.

"Thanks for doing the dishes, Bill. You should have woken me up."

"Hey, no problem. I used the time to think about this case. It is getting really complicated. I know that I discuss aspects of my work with you but this time I cannot. I hope you are going to be okay with that?"

"I do know when something is bothering you but you don't have to worry about me." They enjoyed their breakfast and Bill even had time for a third cup of coffee.

Bill arrived at the station at the same time as Jimmy Moore. "Did you get the court order?" he asked Jimmy.

"Yeah, I explained our problem to Judge Shapiro. He was pretty good about it all. By the way, it really helped that you recognized one of the subjects. There is nothing like hard evidence. So, we are covered for removing all material to the station. He wants to be present when we look at the films with the psychiatrist. If he is still satisfied then he will extend the court order on the films and tapes to whatever date we want. He did say the faster we could clear this up the better it would be. Bill, I want you to get the Pritchard film and audio tapes. We are going to see Dr. Kroeker this morning. I've already notified Judge Shapiro and he will be meeting us at the hospital. We will be using his office conference room and if he is agreeable to be our expert then he will clear his schedule and give us as much time as necessary. Due to the sensitive nature of the audio and films he would prefer to do his work at the hospital instead of the station. As the participants are identified—and they will be identified—he will be able to contact other health care centers on our behalf and that way we can keep this under the radar. He may want to bring in some help but he will run that past us first. For now, it will just be him. Is there anything else that you've thought of?"

"Well, Jimmy, I would like to interview the students who were there when the body was discovered, as well as friends and classmates and roommates and neighbours of Kay Osbourn, Janice Cameron and Beverly Scott. I was thinking about this last night and this morning. In fact I would like to question the three of them again but at the station this time."

"Why the station?" Jimmy asked.

"Because it is not their territory. Also, we can make them feel very uncomfortable. I don't want them feeling safe. I want them to feel threatened. If we can knock them off balance, maybe we will get somewhere. Can it be done without their parents or lawyers being present?"

Jimmy thought about that. "Yeah, it can be done. It might be a little tricky but it can be done. We will just tell them it's an informal procedure and that we need to clear up a few blurred details. Anything else?" he asked.

"You know those appointments Mrs. Poitson arranged?"

"Yes."

"Well, why didn't she include the students who were present when the body was discovered? Do we even know who they are for sure?"

"I'll check the list she provided for me. I just took it for granted that they had no free periods as yet. Mrs. Poitson's list should match with the list that Kay Osbourn provided. You know it really surprised me that Kay Osbourn was so on the ball with putting that list together."

Bill shook his head. "I don't think that the lists will match up. We are going to need to exert some pressure here. We need to see these students and get their story while the story is still fresh in their heads. Once they start talking amongst themselves, details can and will change. Also, I'm curious as to why Kay Osbourn stepped back. Why didn't she go in with the student group? Why wasn't she the first one in to go in after the door was unlocked? What else are we up to today?"

Jimmy replied, "Judge Shapiro will view the film along with Dr. Kroeker. It's all been arranged. He is meeting us at the Grace Hospital this afternoon. In the meantime, let's go and look at the list Mrs. Poitson left for us. If there are names missing between the two lists then we can get her to round up everyone in one spot and then we can interview them. I like your thoughts on Kay Osbourn but I can't help but think you are barking up the wrong tree. I think we'll find out it was someone who took part in the Session Two sessions with Maxwell Meddleton. It would be nice if we could find a list of names and addresses and telephone numbers. It would sure simplify our work. Jimmy was not to know that Dr. Meddleton had destroyed all identifying information. And while I'm thinking of it--no one from Bethesda is to get a look at the films or even listen to the tapes. I don't care how much they scream blue murder."

"No problem, Jimmy. I believe that their intervention could royally screw up this investigation."

CHAPTER 18

Jimmy hauled the list of witnesses from his desk drawer. He and Bill looked it over.

"Some of these names have asterisks. Why? Oh here it is. It's to do with labs. Okay, Bill, let's ask Mrs. Poitson to get everyone together for late this afternoon around 4 pm. It will probably throw a wrench into their weekend plans. Hopefully, we can get through the interviews in a couple of hours. We can grab a bite to eat on the way to the College. Also, I want you to contact Kay, Janice, and Beverly. I want them at the station for 9 am tomorrow. You could ask Mrs. Poitson to get the message to them. Reassure her that it's just details that need clearing up. She'll pass on the reassurance and hopefully they will arrive without any lawyers in tow. Let's get the two films and the two audio tapes. You know what I was wondering?"

"No, Jimmy what?"

"If the films and audio tapes match up for everyone. Or will some of them just be for the first session? The first session being the ones that Janice and Kay knew about. I have a feeling that dear old Maxie kept Session Two very close to his vest as far as information goes. And I am pretty sure that it's the Session Two experience that brought about his death. Also, if we can't locate a master list, how are we going to proceed?"

Bill thought about this for a minute or two and suggested, "That might be something we can ask Judge Shapiro and Dr. Kroeker. I'll go get the films and audio tapes. Do I need to talk to Mrs. Poitson?"

Jimmy nodded. "If she says anything about exams or whatever, just remind her that we need to see those students asap so if they have classes, labs, or exams they will have to be rescheduled. If these kids have labs, hopefully, they are all attending the same labs." Jimmy looked at Bill. "Okay I'll see you in the parking lot in about an hour. Judge Shapiro is taking his own car. We are going to meet him at the Grace for our appointment with Dr. Kroeker."

Bill was almost at the evidence room when he remembered he needed to get the key from the Desk Sergeant. He turned around without hesitation. He needed to know that the first and second sessions films were just that. Based on what he had seen so far, and what Kay Osbourn and Janice Cameron had told him and Jimmy, the Session Two stuff was what was going to concern them the most.

For Jessiman and Moore the ride to the hospital was uneventful. Traffic was exceptionally light and they arrived early for their appointment with Dr. Kroeker and Judge Shapiro.

Detective Moore hoped that talking to Dr. Kroeker beforehand would help him understand what had been happening to these people. He thought it was some kind of mental torture but what did he know. Moore and Jessiman approached the information kiosk and advised the woman that they were there to see Dr. Kroeker. She lifted the handset, waited a moment before hitting the connecting number.

The intercom in Jake's office buzzed. He hit the button, "Jake Kroeker here."

"Dr. Kroeker the detectives are here to see you."

"Send them up please."

The receptionist motioned Moore and Jessiman to the bank of elevators. "It's 4 South, Dr. Kroeker and his associates occupy that wing. They located Dr. Kroeker's office and rapped lightly on the door before walking in. Moore was surprised by the lightness, or rather the brightness, of the room. He looked around and then looked up and saw three skylights. Man, he thought, those skylights are a really nice touch. Not very many windows but the skylights sure let in a tremendous amount of brightness. Jessiman spotted a buzzer on the desk and he gave it a stab with his finger. Jimmy paced the width of the room. He kept rubbing his hands together and then putting them in his pockets, then rubbing his hands together again before putting them back in his pockets. He tried to sit down but was unable to sit and wait. About ten minutes later an inner door opened and Dr. Kroeker stood in the doorway.

"Hi, Jim, I'm ready for you.

"Dr. Kroeker, how are you?" Moore inquired.

"Well, Jim, I thought the uproar from the Milgrim work would have been sufficient to warn others as to acceptable research behavior. I was wrong. I really don't know how this can be contained."

Jimmy remained standing. Jessiman had seated himself by a small table and he had a tape recorder out and his notebook and pen. "Oh yeah, Dr. Kroeker, I forgot to mention we need to tape our sessions with you," Jimmy advised him.

"No problem."

"So what's the story as you see it?" Jimmy asked.

Jake cleared his throat. "Well, I've only viewed the films you left me of the second session. Because I've only seen a couple, my assessment will be based only of the films I've seen. Once you get the all clear on this, I would really like to see all of the first and all of the second session, if you want as complete an assessment as possible. But based on what you left me to view, Dr. Maxwell Meddleton broke every research tenet and possibly several laws as well. I don't believe his work was sanctioned by the College, the Psychological Association, or any other body except Dr. Maxwell Meddleton. However, there is a definite military slant so that is probably where your visitors from the States come in.

"I believe the first sessions were run according to the rules of the day and I don't believe that Dr. Meddleton broke any rules or laws with the first session work. The second session, well, that is something entirely different. Dr. Meddleton used fear, known and unknown, to induce severe psychological trauma. The after effects can show up almost immediately or they could take six months to a year to manifest. It would all depend on the trigger. Exactly what the trigger is, I'm not sure. So far, I have not been able to discern what has taken place in the dark. But once the person encounters whatever it is, then it's game over. To some degree, I don't think Max Meddleton knew what he was doing. I mean he knew what he was doing but he did not know how things were going to play out." Jimmy Moore opened his mouth but Jake Kroeker beat him to it. "I know, not knowing is not a decent defence. By the time I was halfway through I got the impression that Dr. Meddleton knew exactly what he was doing and he was enjoying the suffering and torture his subjects were experiencing. I have several patients who appear to have undergone Meddleton's second session work. I hope once I know what transpired that it would make treating them a lot easier but I don't know. They have been dumped or hung out to dry with no thought as to what they've gone through or will go through. Until I saw these few films I was at a loss as to what brought on the psychosis or psychotic episodes. Even now that I know, I still don't know if I will be able to help them because the trigger or triggers are not recorded or obvious.

Dr. Jake Kroeker was wishing he was far away, far, far away. When this stuff hit the papers all hell was going to break loose. River College was going to be on the hot seat for a long time to come. He had viewed film sequences for those parts of the second sessions that Jimmy Moore had left for him. He was appalled. Dr. Maxwell Meddleton should have been fired from River College and he should have been kicked out of his profession. When all the horrifying details ended up exposed to the hard light of day the media were going to have a field day. River College was going to be in for a very tough time.

"Right now, I believe you need to match up the first and second session participants as quickly as you can. If you can't locate Dr. Meddleton's master list of second session people you will have to interview every participant from the first sessions and question them as to possible participation in the second session. If second session subjects are still outstanding, you will have to advertise to get them to come forward because this is way too serious for anyone to wait for them to come forward on their own. Even waiting for family or friends to start their own inquiry will take far too long. These people needed help yesterday, last month, even a year ago. But, given that has not been possible up to now, then the sooner and better."

"We know, Dr. Kroeker, we know. Jessiman here identified one of Meddleton's subjects for us. It is Sheila Pritchard, the wife of Constable Dennis Pritchard. She has been admitted to the Psych Ward of the General Hospital as of the middle of last week. You may want to get in touch with her physician. Constable Jessiman can give you those details. Dennis is unaware of the underlying circumstances surrounding her admission. He does not know about her participation in Meddleton's work. And all his mother knew was that it was an easy job, did not involve anything illegal, and if it worked out she would have the money she needed to buy Dennis the golf clubs he had been eyeing. He has enough on his plate for the moment. He has two kids. Their only relative is his mother and she is elderly. Apparently,

Sheila had been saving up money and the last of the money she needed probably came from the second session. Pritchard's mom did not know what Sheila was doing but she helped out by babysitting and that involved babysitting overnight for three or four nights. This was all done while Pritchard was away attending a conference. Some of the other wives knew what Sheila was doing in that she would be away for several nights and days but no one else was involved. In fact, one of them had intended to participate but her husband had put his foot down."

Jake Kroeker raised his eyebrows and Jimmy responded.

"It's a long story. He really loves his wife. I guess he's happy she really did listen to him this time. I can arrange for you to see the first sessions films, along with the corresponding audio tapes as soon as Judge Shapiro gives us the all clear to go ahead. That will be sorted out today. Jake, the people you have helping you—do they understand that we don't need a leak to the newspapers? What we really don't need is a wholesale panic."

Jake nodded. "You won't have a problem with any of my residents. However, I will have to report this breach of ethics and the harmful outcome to the psychological and psychiatric Associations and to River College as well. Once that happens I don't see any of this staying under wraps. I'll try to hold off for as long as possible. Hopefully, we'll have the subjects from the second session identified. Those we can't identify, well, it will probably have to be a public appeal. I don't see any other way."

CHAPTER 19

"How is it going with the Bethesda people?" Jake asked.

Jimmy and Jessiman grinned. "Thank God our judges were not easily intimidated or scared off by the crap these guys were handing out. We had to show several judges a couple of tapes—we showed them the first and second sessions with Sheila Pritchard. The second was a young man but he hasn't been identified as yet. I swear, their non-existent hair stood on end. They sure made short shrift of those bozos. They are cooling their heels. I have suggested that we will contact them when our investigation has been completed, so if they want they can go back where they came from. So far, they do not appear to have taken my advice seriously." Jimmy was silent for several moments, then he asked, "Dr. Kroeker, is there any way we'll ever find out who or what was behind this? I mean, do you really think Dr. Meddleton dreamed this up on his own?"

Jake was silent for several moments and then he sighed. "Near as I can see he designed the second session portion himself. I'm not positive but I don't think everyone was subjected to the same degree as the constable's wife or the young man. I'm sure there will be others. Dr. Meddleton knew what the Bethesda people wanted and he aimed to please. I think what he designed here is by far more unethical than anything that's been done to date. He answered to no one and there was no oversight of any kind. That kind of freedom or license to operate usually gives birth to really outrageous, even dangerous situations. Were you able to track down that fellow from the first session? You know, the Teutonic fellow with the huge hands."

Jessiman and Moore nodded an affirmative. Jimmy Moore spoke up. "My money was on Gunther. He's strong enough to have carried out the stabbing but he has an iron clad alibi and unless we can prove he is lying we are out of luck. Also, he never took part in the second sessions so what would have been his motive?

"We need to find those subjects fast. Dead is no good to us. Dead will get you into the papers," Jake Kroeker replied with a qualifying statement.

"There are still twenty-two subjects outstanding. Of the ones we've been able to match up at least eighteen have died, usually by their own hand. What I've done is sent out a letter to all the psych hospitals requesting information on any patients who resided here in the city or province for the last three years. These people would be exhibiting self-destructive behaviours as well as unusual and uncontrollable phobic fears that came on without warning and did not appear to have an obvious cause or etiology. And, if we cannot track these missing ones there could be many more deaths to deal with. What makes it more difficult is that the triggers or what sets them off appears to be different for all the subjects. It would have made it so much easier if Meddleton had kept a master list."

Jessiman nodded in agreement. "We've gone through every piece of paper, every audio tape for the first session as well as the filmed sequences. We're just starting on the Session Two daytime tapes and we still have the filmed sequences of Session Two to match up to their respective audio sessions. Do you think he even intended for anyone to be able to trace these individuals?"

Dr. Kroeker responded with a shake of his head. "You know, Jessiman, you've nailed it. If there is no master list we are up the creek without a paddle. But what makes this really difficult is the fact that we know when the participants ran into trouble in the pod in the dark but we don't know what set them off. And, what set them off is probably the triggering effect. But unless you are with them when they snap the trigger remains a mystery."

CHAPTER 20

There Was Never Any Oversight

According to the reception girl on the main floor, Judge Shapiro still had not arrived. Dr. Kroeker had asked that someone accompany the judge to his office but things and events were known to slip up if the reception area got busy so he left his connecting door to the outer office open. Jimmy cleared his throat.

"Well, Jake, have you been able to reach any conclusions regarding the audio tape and film that I left for you to look over?" Dr. Kroeker frowned. His fingers met in front of his chin as if in prayer.

"I would rather wait for Judge Shapiro to see what we have here but I can tell you this much. Meddleton was messing with their minds big time. Do you know that we've got several people in the secure section who cannot tolerate any degree of darkness? The lights have to left on in their room at all times. I'm wondering if we will find them on one of his tapes and I'm beginning to believe that it is a given, a done deal. Have you been able to locate any sort of list at all?

Jimmy replied with a shake of his head. "No, but we are working on it." Just then they heard the outer office door open and close. Dr. Kroeker got up from his desk and went into the outer office.

"Judge Shapiro?"

"Yes, you must be Dr. Kroeker?"

"Just call me Jake. Please come in. Detective Moore and Constable Jessiman are in my office."

The introductions were brief. Dr. Kroeker motioned for Bill to close the door. Then he drew the blinds. He wheeled a small projector and tape machine from the corner of his office.

"We won't need a screen because the wall on this side will do quite nicely. I think we should view the tapes first and then listen to the audio. I do not recommend running them both at the same time." He switched on the film projector. They sat in absolute silence. Dr. Kroeker noticed that Jessiman had his hand over his eyes as if to shield them. Jimmy Moore sat stiffly and the only movement was his cracking of his knuckles. Then the film ended.

Judge Shapiro cleared his throat. "You know I already saw some of this when the warrants were approved. How many more of these do I have to watch?"

Jimmy answered, "Only as many as you need to for your decision on the court order impounding these materials so that we can keep on with our investigation. If we have to give the audio tapes and filmed sequences to the American investigators our investigation will be incomplete because the evidence is contained on the audio tapes and the films. Right now this is all we have. However, I have one more set of tapes that I asked Bill to retrieve from the station. This set hits close to home because the victim is the wife of one of the members of our force.

Judge Shapiro appeared to be reluctant but finally gave a nod to Dr. Kroeker to put in another reel. By the time it ran its course the judge was perspiring profusely. He appeared to be unnaturally pale.

"That's enough. I need some time before I listen to the audio tapes. Please excuse my language but how the fuck did this person get away with this?"

Jimmy answered. "We don't know yet, Judge Shapiro, but we are working on it. If it helps, the audio tapes are not quite as horrendous mainly because we cannot see what is happening. That is not to say that they aren't awful in their own right. We'll play at least two for you." He nodded to Jake to start the reel-to-reel tape machine.

The silence in the room was broken by a series of unidentifiable sounds. A low guttural moaning which increased in timbre until it was a full-fledged scream. A loud thud was heard and then the silence broken only by a creaking sound. Finally, they could hear some movement and then a voice which they believed to be Dr. Meddleton's. He was talking to himself while his subject was out for the count. It sounded like he was admonishing Sheila for not having gone the distance. He referred to her chicken heart a number of times. Finally, a silence fell on the room and the listeners.

Judge Shapiro cleared his throat. He appeared to be having difficulty speaking. "How many of these do we have to listen to?"

"Just a couple," Jimmy answered. "But I think you

should pick the next one that we listen to so that later on we cannot be accused of bias." He opened up the binders. "Help yourself."

"Is there any way to determine the dates of these recordings?" Judge Shapiro asked. "The last one I understand is fairly recent. What about an earlier one?"

Jimmy nodded to Bill to answer the judge's query.

"We have not catalogued everything as yet. These binders were in Dr. Meddleton's office at River College. His technicians referred to Session One and Session Two material. Neither of them had anything to do with Session Two itself, however, Meddleton was planning on having them assist when he started to view the Session Two tapes. Apparently, they viewed Session One for both day and night. But viewing of daytime Session Two was very recent. In fact, the senior technician said that she only found out very recently from Dr. Meddleton that the Session Two participants did not have access to a panic button. They had never viewed the nighttime sessions of Session Two. It was the daytime behaviour of one or two of the subjects that concerned them the most. At least that is what one of them told us."

Jimmy spoke up. "It is the Session Two material that the Bethesda people want possession of. We believe all the material from Session Two is central to this investigation, Your Honour. Just before you arrived, Dr. Kroeker informed us that he had or knew of several patients on the secure ward that could not tolerate any degree of darkness at all. The lights in the room for these patients have to remain on at all times. He believes the answer to their situation may be found in these tapes."

Judge Shapiro stood up and walked over the desk where the binders lay. He selected a tape from the middle of the binder. "Okay, let's get this over with." Instead of returning to his chair, he went over and stood by the window. He knew he was being silly but that little sliver of light showing at the edges of the blinds was necessary to him at this precise moment. Once again the silence in the room was broken by more unidentifiable sounds. "Rats! Those noises are rats!" Judge Shapiro exclaimed. He motioned to Jake to stop the tape.

"What you are trying to tell me is that these people listened to this in total darkness? Jesus! This guy would have been at home at Buchenwald or any other concentration camp that the Nazis ran during World War II." He nodded to Jake to restart the tape. He could recognize the escalating terror in the noises the subject made and he was also able to recognize the precise instant that the subject lost consciousness by the scream that was cut off in an instant, followed by a thud on the floor. The ensuing silence was broken by the creaking of a door and Dr. Meddleton's whisper about the subject's efforts and how they hadn't lasted long enough. Judge Shapiro stayed beside the window with its sliver of light and his hand kept contact with the blind and its tremble was evidenced by the bouncing sliver of light that came and went in the room.

Bill Jessiman stood up and walked over to the door and flicked the lights on. He noticed that everyone in the room appeared to take a deep breath, actually several deep breaths.

Judge Shapiro pulled the blind up at the window where he was standing.

"Gentlemen, I'll give you a court order to cover the material from Meddleton's lab and office. I'm going one step further and am including his home in the order. If those Americans are on their way here I would suggest that you get everything removed to a secure place. This court order supersedes the earlier one you were given and will cover you for five months but at some point you will require an extension. In time my decision will be overridden and you will have to give them access to the audio and the films. When that time comes I would suggest giving them copies and keeping the originals. If we get to trial on this, it will be important to have the originals, not copies." He opened his briefcase, took out a leather folder, opened it, and removed several printed pages. He took the top off his fountain pen and filled in location, names, and dates as required. He took a stamp out of his briefcase and forcefully applied it to the last page. He indicated to Dr. Kroeker that he should witness the document. That done, he handed the original over to Jimmy Moore and he indicated to Dr. Kroeker that the copy had to be witnessed as well. The copy was returned to the leather folder and then the folder was returned to his briefcase and he snapped it shut.

Judge Shapiro cleared his throat. "I know Meddleton's murder was in the paper. How long before the other details get published? By details, I mean the Session Two experiments. That's what they were, you know. Experiments."

Jimmy spoke up. "The media won't get any further

information from our office. However, at some point we may need to track everyone down. I can tell you this much. You will be kept informed of any and all developments as they happen. Thank you for backing us up, Your Honour." Judge Shapiro shook hands with Jimmy Moore and Bill Jessiman. He went over to Dr. Kroeker. They spoke together for several minutes, then shook hands and Judge Shapiro turned, picked up his overcoat and briefcase. He walked out the door into the waiting room. They heard the outer door close behind him.

"Well, Bill, let's get this show on the road. Let's see if these search orders can be executed before those Bethesda folk get here." He and Bill smiled at each other. "We'll call you later on, Jake. If anything new turns up at this end will you let us know?"

"No problem, Jimmy. I'll maintain patient confidentiality but I will keep you appraised as to the treatment progress. You know…" Jake paused for a moment. "I know you have a murderer to catch but believe it or not this guy did us a favour. Who knows how much worse this could have been—and it is pretty bad right now but at least Meddleton is out of commission."

Jimmy nodded in agreement and said, "Murder is murder. There is no excuse for murder. There should have been another solution. Murder is never the solution. It just compounds the problem."

CHAPTER 21

Early Autumn

The investigation into the murder of Dr. Maxwell Meddleton had entered the sixth month and appeared to have ground to a halt. They had interviewed everyone from Session One and as many as could be traced from the Session Two scheduled appointments. They had had to resort to some under-handedness on their part to track down the Session Two participants. A fire at the lab and offices had been engineered. In order to "save" years of painstaking research, people were asked to assist the College by reporting if they had taken part in any work sponsored by several researchers including Dr. Maxwell Meddleton. At first, they believed the ruse was not going to work but suddenly people began to come forth. The really awful part turned out to be the relatives or friends of participants in Meddleton's work. A large number of suicides were reported as well as several murders. What really surprised them all was the fact that one of the Session Two participants was occupying a bed in the Psychiatric Ward at the Vancouver General Hospital. How she had been tracked down was still a mystery.

The College's cooperation was what could only be called half-hearted. The dean kept jabbering about "right of research" and "confidentiality" and that old horse "the research ethic." The Bethesda people had been like a room of circus performers on a high wire who had had their net removed when they were not looking. They had questioned the two technicians several times and they had called Beverly Scott in for questioning even though she was not a suspect. The only thing they did find out was that Beverly's affair with Max Meddleton was not the secret she thought it was.

In the course of the investigation, Kay had reported Dr. Meddleton's concern with one of the Session One participants, Gunther Hiebert. They had been unable to break his alibi. In fact, of all of them, Hiebert's alibi had been the one that was airtight. Weird. He was strong enough to have killed Meddleton with his bare hands but—and it was a big but—Hiebert had been out of town for several days which included the weekend of the murder. Apparently, the money for the weekend was from Dr. Meddleton and Kay did confirm that when she reported the last conversation she had with Dr. Meddleton. All the students who had been present when the body was discovered had been questioned several times. No one seemed to think it strange that Kay had not entered the room before any of them. She had unlocked the door and then was intent on getting back to the library, just like she did whenever she was not scheduled to work with them. It was not her shift and she was just letting them in. Same as always. It was the screams of the students that had alerted her to the fact that something was wrong. She had maintained an amazing calm. In fact, the list of students present when Dr. Meddleton's body was discovered was due to Kay. She thought the police might need to know just who exactly was there so she made a note of everyone's name and their home phone number.

It also took extra time to cross-reference all the lists of subjects which included their lists, the lists received from Mrs. Poitson, and several lists from Kay Osbourn and Janice. The administration's cooperation was not whole-hearted. The Americans were still on site but were not as officious or offensive as they had been at the start of the investigation.

They were still transcribing Dr. Meddleton's notes for themselves and the Americans. The investigation was costing a fortune in collateral expenses. They had tons of paper which translated into tons of investigative paperwork and hundreds maybe even thousands of interviews, if anyone had been keeping count. Everything from the lab, Meddleton's office, the Black Room or the Pod, and everything in Meddleton's home had been catalogued. That is what they had taken to referring to Meddleton's work among themselves. The Black Room.

Dean Sullivan had been felled by a heart attack and a new dean had been added to the mix. Mrs. Poitson had retired and they were dealing with a new administrative assistant. Miss Bennette did dress well and her dimness was not openly obvious, but over time it had become apparent that she was not the brightest bulb in the room. She had also tried to derail the investigation by supplying incomplete data searches, etc. She had no reason for this behaviour, just sheer bloody mindedness on her part. All her behaviour accomplished was that Jimmy went directly to the dean or department head and cut her out of the picture. Miss Bennette was not a happy camper!

Dr. Jake Kroeker had done extensive research and investigation into Meddleton's work. Most of what he had accessed was innocuous, really, really boring even, but there were a number of papers that probably heralded the direction Meddleton's work was taking if anyone had thought to ask the right questions of him. Jake had not come across anything definitive linking Bethesda to the research. It was the consensus at this point that if the Americans had stayed out of it no one would have been any wiser. Instead, a major political pot was boiling over. Canadian and American politicians were united in shutting the barn door after the horse had escaped.

Jake particularly found the paper *Darkness and Silence* very revealing in its conclusions, bearing in mind that they now knew what Meddleton had been up to and the mind games he had designed and orchestrated for the American research group.

> *"In summary, we can conclude that exposing subjects to prolonged darkness and silence can result in perceptual changes, appearance of hallucinatory-type experiences, changes in emotionality, impairment of recent memory, and significant changes in EEG activity, all of which point to considerable disorganization of brain function."* Under these conditions the

> *activity of the brain may be impaired and disturbances of psychological processes my occur."*

Jake knew without a doubt that if Dr. Meddleton had confined his experiments to basic sensory deprivation of a short duration as was done in his earlier work, the psychological fallout would have been close to nonexistent. It was the addition of the unknown noises, the sudden shocks administered by Dr. Meddleton in the total darkness of the Black Room that pushed them over the edge. As far as Jake was concerned whoever had taken Dr. Meddleton out had performed an outstanding service. God only knew how many souls had been lost because of Max Meddleton's work. The patient in the psych ward of Vancouver General was beginning to show signs of coming around but it was going to take a long, long time and the bottom line was that she might never be normal again. The number of participants in the second session was frightening in the number of deaths that had been the eventual outcome. What was even more shocking was the number of suicides that had been tracked back to Meddleton's Session Two experiments.

CHAPTER 22

It All Begins to Come Together

Jake had tracked down a paper from Meddleton's early research that he believed was the harbinger of the Bethesda involvement. The comments within that paper had his hair standing on end.

> "Furthermore, in the case of both recall and recognition, the experimental subjects still exhibited a significant impairment one day after isolation ($p = .05$)." Intellectual Changes During Isolation (Darkness & Silence). "In experiments where no restriction on movements are applied, hallucinatory phenomena seem to be totally or almost absent, while in experiments such as ours where the subject is requested to restrict his movements inside the chamber, hallucinatory activity seems to be quite common

Bill Jessiman was on his way home. He had stopped off

to do some errands for Donna. He was headed for the cashier just as he noticed the headline on the front page of the River City Tribune. Normally, he would not bother getting a paper but the headline grabbed his attention—"Investigation Concludes River City College Science Student Jumped to Death from Fortune Street Bridge." He had to read through most of the story before the student was identified. David Carter. Bill was sure that a David Carter had taken part in Session Two. He was positive that the body he and Matt had retrieved prior to his assignment to Jimmy Moore had eventually been identified as David Carter. He needed to get back to the station and check the lists again. He paid for his purchases and almost forgot to pay for the paper. He also checked the obituary page but the only mention of any service was that it was going to be a Memorial Service on campus. It appeared that David Carter had no family. They were still tracking down Session Two participants but he was sure he would find David Carter on a list somewhere. He made a note of the time and date of the service. If he was right, then Jimmy needed to know right away and their search parameters would be expanded to all the students and not just the general public. That was something else to add to his "to do" list. How many of the Session Two participants had been students? Was that why they had not been able to track everyone down? They were students, not just ordinary working stiffs! He would need to list the names not yet tracked down and compare it with the student lists. The College would be screaming again no doubt, but it seemed to Jessiman that someone should have been screaming at and about Maxwell Meddleton a long time ago.

Bill arrived at the station. He had made one stop and that was to call Donna so she wouldn't worry when he didn't arrive home on time. Checking out the names might take a couple of hours. He located the binder with the Session Two names. He was beginning to feel like he knew their contents backwards and forwards. There it was—DB62. Now, where was the list of the names of the participants. He opened several more binders and then he saw it: David C, Age 24, Biochemistry Major. He would have his work cut out for him to prove or disprove a connection but in his bones he knew he was onto something. He picked up the phone to call Detective Moore at home with his news. Bill was really glad to have something positive to tell Jimmy. He knew Jimmy was worried that the investigation seemed to be going nowhere with no positive outcome. After he spoke with Jimmy, he made himself a cup of coffee and opened up one of the four Session Two binders and made a separate list of any outstanding case exemplars. He did the same for the other three binders. Then he took the list of names and beginning with David Carter, he attempted to match the independent list of names to the case exemplars. Several weeks back he had spent days and days going through obituary notices beginning around the time the Session Two runs were thought to have begun. Now, he had his list of case exemplars with possible matching names and he was comparing this to the listing of death notices.

The work required total concentration and took Jessiman several hours. Jessiman put everything away but he was satisfied that maybe, just maybe, another half dozen or more case exemplars had been paired with a name and matched with an obituary notice in either major newspaper. He would have to follow all of it up it the next day or two. Tomorrow, he and Jimmy Moore would return to River College and request a master list of student names across the board for at least three years. With any luck they might be able to knock a few more names off the unknown list.

Everyone, including the College, was trying to keep everything low key and off of the newspapers radar. No one, especially the College and the Canadian Government, wanted this to get out and become water cooler fodder. The American investigators had spent days with the cities transcriptionists and they were finally out of their hair. They were not happy because they only had copies. They had wanted all the original material but Judge Shapiro's ruling had put a spoke in the works and his ruling had held up over several court challenges. In a private meeting, Judge Shapiro had delicately implied that perhaps his good friend Walter Werner from the Tribune needed to be in on this. It would make quite a story! That had shut the American investigators up and they were now out of the picture. Once the investigation was completed Bill supposed the College would retain ownership of the original materials. Bill's private thoughts were that the college was attempting to keep a considerable distance between Dr. Meddleton's research and the investigation into his death. In no way, did they want anyone making a connection that went from his research to his untimely death. So far, they had done well. Only time would tell.

CHAPTER 23

In Memory Of

Kay Osbourn had attended the service for David Carter along with dozens of other students and professors. Only she, the detectives, and the College administration knew that David's death was linked to Maxwell Meddleton's research. She wasn't even sure if Janice Cameron, her co-worker, had made the connection. Kay kept waiting for the proverbial axe to fall which would have resulted in her arrest. Nothing. Nothing happened. Days, weeks, months had passed. Then it was one year, two years, and then five years and now twenty years later. The murder of Dr. Maxwell Meddleton remained open. Kay was always on edge.

Detective Jimmy Moore had been promoted several times and was now retired. Bill Jessiman was now a Lieutenant in the homicide division. He and Kay had met up several months back. He had driven down to Carberry to go over details of the case that was still open and unsolved. Kay was getting tired of these infrequent visits from the law. All they succeeded in doing was opening up old wounds. Wounds that were not allowed to heal or even scab over. It was tremendously nerve wracking to keep all the details straight and her answers the same. She had finally written everything they asked down and made a note of her answers. By reviewing these notes she was able to keep herself from tripping up.

She was glad that the surviving Session Two subjects were all provided with free counseling and free pharmaceutical care courtesy of the Canadian Government and the Americans. There had only been three other suicides after Dr. Meddleton had been dispatched. The wife of the city policeman, Sheila Pritchard, was doing reasonably well but it had taken years of therapy.

All Kay had, to remind her of what could have been, was a ring. David had left a package for her with the resident housemother. Kay had not received the package until months after the funeral. The housemother had put it away and had forgotten all about it. It was all so bittersweet and futile. If only David had listened to her, maybe they would have had a future together. Kay had found the most recent visit from Bill Jessiman to be totally upsetting. She did not know why but she felt like her days were numbered.

The last two years had been particularly harrowing. Her parents were both gone. Her father's death was a complete shock to her and her mom. Then her mom got the Big C diagnosis and was advised that she had about a year. She was gone within six months. It had taken Kay quite a while to begin feeling normal again. Whatever normal was. The farm was hers and she rented out the land and was free to dabble in whatever interested her. On an impulse she visited the travel agency in Brandon. Winter was on its way and she wanted to go somewhere where they didn't know what snow and freezing rain were. She had a number of pamphlets and had to make up her mind. Her choices were Australia, New Zealand, Fiji, Malaysia, Sri Lanka, and Thailand. Europe was out because snow, freezing rain and floods were less of an aberration and becoming more of the norm. Right now, she was wavering between New Zealand and Thailand. Money was not a problem but she did want her money's worth. Her community work kept her out of trouble. Thanks to the revenue from the farm, she did not need to work a nine to five job. At least her mom and dad had gotten to see her get her PhD. So, she was Dr. Osbourn, not that it did her much good. She did not want to involve herself in anything and then get arrested, so she felt it was better to hole herself off. She kept herself busy by tutoring students and supervising an English as a second language course at River College. She kept a small but cozy apartment in River City and came home to the farm on weekends.

Her love life was basically nonexistent. There was no point in getting involved with anyone and then screwing things up by being arrested. There had been a few guys over the last twenty years but the ground rules were made clear from the start—there would not be any long-term relationships, no strings, no ties, no partnerships. Either could call it quits and it was usually Kay who pulled the plug. She realized she needed to get away and the sooner the better. She wrote her destination choices down on scraps of paper. She tossed them into a bowl and, without looking, took one out, turned it face down and tacked it to the dart board on the back of the kitchen door. She did the same with the other slips of paper. Then she mixed herself a tall gin and tonic. She took a long sip and savoured the flavors as they enveloped her mouth. God, but it was sure good!

She got her darts out. Then she stood back and thought about what she was doing. She threw the first dart. Then she had another long drink. She walked over and put on a rock CD, came back, and threw another dart at the board. The phone rang, and she answered.

"Kay Osbourn here. Yes...yes...I understand. No, I am not interested in being interviewed! I don't give a damn what anniversary date it is. I am through being interviewed!"

Kay slammed the phone down. This was never going to end. She picked up another dart and heaved it at the board. She took another drink. Her glass was empty. She helped herself to another gin and tonic and carried it over to where the last three darts awaited. She propped her ass against the counter and took another drink. Then she threw dart number four. Darts five and six followed. She took her glass and went and sat down on the sofa. She could wait until morning to see where she was going. The last dart was the deciding throw. It had needed to be as close to the target center and as close to a destination paper as possible. The destinations were all face down on the dart board. Morning would reveal all.

CHAPTER 24

Kay walked down the stairs and into the kitchen. She put the coffee on. What should she have for breakfast this morning? She decided on whole wheat toast and honey, some fresh fruit and a couple of chunks of cheddar cheese. She walked to the front door and got the daily paper out of the mailbox. Then she returned to the kitchen. Her coffee was ready. She poured herself a cup and topped it off with some half and half. She put bread in the toaster and sipped her coffee while she waited for the toaster to pop. The toast popped and Kay buttered the slices with homemade butter and a healthy dollop of honey on each slice. She saved the cheddar cheese. The best for last!

Kay planned to stop off at the travel agency later. She still did not know where she would be headed for her winter vacation. She would check the dart board before she left to meet with her travel agent. She was somewhat surprised that she was neither curious nor excited about her mystery destination. She put away her breakfast things and rinsed her coffee cup. The phone rang interrupting her solitude. She picked up the receiver and listened for a moment and then hung up without responding to the caller. If they called back she was just going to lay the receiver down and hang it back up when she got back home. It was amazing how absolutely aggravating journalists and the media were.

She made sure her doors were locked before she went upstairs to get dressed. She selected a nifty dress she had found at Eveline Street in Lockport. She decided on a really cute pair of sandals and transferred her things from one handbag to another. Her jewelry of choice today was a minimalist design from Heather of Gypsy Jewels. Kay took a final look in the full-length mirror and headed back downstairs. She went over to the dartboard and picked up her digital camera that was sitting on the counter. She took a picture of the location of the darts and destination papers on the dartboard. She removed the dart and paper that were actually the closest together. Then she took a second photo. The photos were her way of ensuring she did not cheat on the location or final destination. Past experience guaranteed the decision to go with the darts. The only time she had had a problem was when she had not followed the choice of the darts. That was a holiday never to be forgotten.

She turned her destination paper over—Thailand. Well, now she knew where she was going. She walked out the front door and went around the corner to the carport. She loved her convertible. Kay got in and turned the key. The engine started up and even though it had not been anywhere for a while, it sounded great. Her convertible was for country driving and lots of times it was with the top down. Even if the weather was a bit off there was still nothing like it. When she had to return to River College and her work in the city she kept a Ford sedan for city driving. There was less chance of the Ford being stolen on the city streets. She drove the convertible out of the carport and took the circular drive to the access road in front of the farm. From there, it was a twenty-minute drive to Highway 1 and then west to Brandon. She remembered that she had not called first to make sure her travel agent was in. The trip itself would be done so that she would be spending Christmas in Thailand and not returning until the end of January. Her neighbours would keep an eye on her home. She had no animals, domesticated or otherwise, to look after so they would not have too much to do. Just make sure the pipes did not freeze, electricity stayed on and no break-ins. She parked her car and walked toward the travel agency. She really liked their new location. Previously, the agency had been in a mall. The mall was not conducive to one-on-one consultations. Outside it was noisy with kids yelling, crying, or just make noise in general. The cubicles assigned to each agent were minuscule and there was no real accommodation for private conversations.

The new location was on the third floor of an old five story refurbished block. The views from their windows was marvellous. The building had elevator service. The elevators were the old style consisting of a wrought iron cage that was mirrored. They were so cool, so elegant. The offices were really nice with spaces on the walls for travel posters and room for a couple of comfortable easy chairs, a computer, printer and filing cabinet. There were at least two shelves that held travel mementos collected by the agent or given to her by a client.

Kay had found a parking spot on the street. Her trip on the elevator only took a couple of minutes.

"Hi Jill, is Sandra in?"

"No, Dr. Osbourn, she won't be in until later this afternoon. Probably closer to 2:30 or 3:00 pm. Is there anything I can help you with?" Jill asked.

"Well, I do have some other errands I can run, Jill. Would you mind telling Sandra that my next trip will be to Thailand? I want to leave around the twelfth or fifteenth of December and I want to be back in Brandon by the end of the first week in February. Also, I do not want to stay in a large center except for three or four days before I return home. I feel I need to get away completely to unwind. Actually, I won't be back today, perhaps you can give me an appointment for the middle of the week or on Saturday. Whichever works out best."

"Sure, Dr. Osbourn. Let me get Sandra's appointment book."

"Thanks, Jill, I appreciate this very much."

When Kay left she had an appointment for one in the afternoon on Wednesday. Jill had blocked off two or three hours for Kay and Sandra. Kay drove around and got her other errands done. She visited the bank and requested access to her safety deposit box and she also asked to use a small corner room to check over her documents.

CHAPTER 25

First, she looked her passport over. It would not expire for another two years. So, everything was in order for this trip. She opened an envelope and removed the handwritten pages. She read them over. There were no changes to make so she initialized, signed, and dated the missive again. Next, she took out the envelope labeled *Last Will and Testament*. She read that over very carefully. Then she put everything back except for the will which she refolded and placed in her handbag. She would need to make an appointment with her lawyer. Her will had not been revised or updated since her graduation well before her parents had passed away. She locked up and waited for the assistant to return to do her job to secure the locked box and return it to its proper slot.

Kay stopped in at the public library and took out several books on Thailand. Her last stop was at her favourite deli and coffee shop. Her shopping was done and now it was time for a treat. She ordered an extra-large caramel macchiato with extra whipped cream and chocolate drizzle and nutmeg. She did not order anything to eat. The coffee was her treat for today.

She found a quiet corner and took out the smaller missive on Thailand that she had put in her purse. For the next hour or so she sipped her coffee and studied the text on Thailand. She came to the realization that avoiding the big city meant something on the coast or inland from the coast. More than likely a resort town. She thought about this and decided that a resort might not be too bad after all. She always travelled by herself and she always booked a suite. Sure, the suite was a bit extravagant but it gave her the privacy she craved.

Kay returned to River City College after the weekend. She had things to do before everything was finalized for the trip. Her will had to be updated and she needed to make sure her English as a Second Language students were comfortable with her replacement and she had to make sure that they did not sign up for any research projects without running the details past her or her replacement. There would never be a repeat of the Meddleton fiasco ever again. She had also endured several days of phone inquiries from television and radio personalities but those requests had died a natural death. She wanted nothing more to do with rehashing all that had happened years ago. She was done with it.

When confirmation of the identity of the body pulled from the Red River was made and it turned out to be David Carter she had felt that she had died as well. In fact, she had come pretty close to confessing her part in Meddleton's death but something had held her back. Now, here it was, twenty years later and still no one on the investigative team had tied her to any of it. Kay had decided that she needed to make another change before she left on her holiday. She was going to give up her apartment in Osborne Village. She would store her stuff in the insulated shed on the farm and when she returned she would look for another apartment. An apartment with a few more modern comfort amenities but with some extra's like a gym and an indoor pool/ Closer to shopping, the theatre, art galleries and museum. She still had a few years to go before retirement. The ESL program was not onerous and she enjoyed her contact with the students. It was amazing to see how they improved over time and how their command of English went from rudimentary to very, very good and it only took a few years of hard work on their part.

Once Kay had made up her mind she moved quickly. A van was hired and she enlisted extra helping hands from several young men in the program. They were paid very well for their efforts and they got to see some extra countryside when they drove the van from Winnipeg to her home in Carberry. The furniture was in storage on the farm. When she returned from her vacation she would decide if she was keeping it or donating it to the Salvation Army or Mennonite Central. Both organizations did excellent work. Now that things were actually happening Kay was beginning to get a bit excited about her upcoming trip. She knew she would be visiting several of her favourite shops to augment her holiday wardrobe.

CHAPTER 26

Phuket, Thailand…Here I Come!

All the travel arrangements had been taken care of with the help of Sandra her travel agent and her assistant Jill. The return ticket was paid for, the resort town of Phuket was her destination of choice, and she would be spending at least three days in Singapore before returning to Vancouver and then finally home to Brandon via Air Canada. She had seen her lawyer and updated her will and she had a copy with her. Her will and the letter sealed in a separate envelope were not going to be left behind this trip. She felt more in control and felt it was a better idea to have them with her rather than leaving them behind in the safety deposit box. She perused the resort pamphlets. It was going to be perfect!

She would be staying in a private cottage that fronted the beach. It had a living or sitting room, bathroom, bedroom, and a corner for a microwave and coffee maker and toaster. The bedroom had a queen-sized bed. A veranda ran the whole front of the cottage. She did not have to do any cooking. After all, coffee and toast and a scrambled egg did not constitute cooking in the traditional sense of the word. She just had to stroll over to the hotel dining room.

There were several pools of different sizes and for different swimming abilities. There was even a tidal pool that looked unique. The colours in the travel brochures that Sandra had given her were absolutely stunning—the really bright, deep greens, outstanding blues and every colour in between!

Kay drove her sedan to Winnipeg. She overnighted in a hotel close to the airport. She was leaving her car in the long-term parking area. The hotel would provide a vehicle to get her to the airport for her 4 am flight. Going through International Customs added some extra strain to her travels. It would be a long drawn-out procedure before getting to step on the plane even though it was only to Vancouver with a two hour layover before catching the connecting flight to Singapore and then a boat to Phuket in Thailand. She would arrive in Thailand on December fifteenth.

The layover in Vancouver was uneventful. The next leg was very long and Singapore was reached very late on the night of the second day of travel. A hotel had been arranged for and Kay finally fell asleep with the sounds of the city coming through the open window. She slept very well and woke up about 1 pm completely rested. The trip to Phuket by ship would commence at 4 pm and they would reach the resort early the next morning.

Kay had a light meal in the hotel restaurant and she also purchased some fruit from a street vendor along with several bottles of water that had a label that she recognized and would require some supersized strength to open. She intended to wash the fruit before she left the hotel. She only had her carry-on bag to worry about. Her checked luggage was taken care of by the resort personnel who had offloaded their identified bags to a trolley from the plane and then to a truck for the trip to Phuket.

Kay boarded the SUV at the hotel and they arrived at the quay having driven through more crowds and more traffic than she had ever seen. The noise! Sure, it was the middle of the day but the level of noise, the conglomeration of people, and the assault of sounds was like nothing she had ever experienced! She left the SUV and stood in a line along with everyone else and presented her ticket and showed her passport to the government official. Her passport was stamped and she walked up the ramp to the section of ship where everyone was congregated. She stood at the railing gazing down at all the activity. Ropes were untied and the ship began to move away from the dock. Her vacation was officially underway! Kay conversed with several couples and made plans to join them for dinner. She was on holiday and so was everyone else. Why be stuck-up or unfriendly and cause someone unhappiness and possibly ruin their day?

At some point during dinner she became aware of a feeling that she was being watched. It was difficult to tell who was causing her unease. After dinner, she excused herself and made her way back to her cabin. She lay down on the bunk and dozed off. She awoke once or twice but went back to sleep quite quickly. When the horn finally sounded and the cabin porter knocked on her door to tell her they had arrived at Phuket, she was ready.

She looked over the railing at the beach where their runabout boat would take them. The view was absolutely stunning! It was warm—not killer hot, just wonderfully warm. It was heaven! She had purchased several postcards at the hotel in Singapore and they were addressed and ready to mail before she got off the ship. Several were for her ESL students, one was for Sandra, and one for Jill. Another was for the couple looking after her house and property. She dropped the postcards into the ship's mailbox and then walked over to where everyone was waiting patiently for their turn to board the runabout. The line was moving not too bad and soon it would be her turn.

She became aware of an older fellow behind her. *Good mornings* were exchanged and he asked, "Is this resort your destination or are you headed further down the coast?"

"No, I'll be getting off here." Kay did not ask him where he was going. She did not care. Then it was her turn to disembark from the ship. The older fellow did not follow. Instead he moved out of line and motioned for the next two couples to move up.

Kay clambered up to the dock from the runabout and then strolled down the dock to the beach and the path to the resort. My God, this was an absolutely, unbelievably beautiful place! The sounds of the birds, the voices all round, and the different languages that she eventually became aware of, along with the smell of the sea and sand. She knew she was going to love her time here.

Kay took advantage of some of the day trips that had been laid on. Each one was an exhilarating experience. The locals that she met were so friendly and happy and helpful. She ate in the hotel restaurant at night and was invited to join different couples and families. While she preferred to eat on her own she did join up for dessert and/or drinks afterwards. Holiday acquaintances were beneficial to experiencing a happy holiday. Tonight she was joining the fellow from their ship, Daniel Gregor. She had spoken with him just prior to getting off at Phuket. She had taken a train excursion further inland. It was a day trip and they had run into each other while visiting a temple. He seemed to be a decent sort. He did not appear to be looking for a bed partner which pleased her even more. They planned on having dinner together at her resort and then would get together again for an early morning swim and breakfast. Their dinner was excellent. The band played terrific dance music. Being with Daniel was a lot of fun. The whole evening was perfect.

Kay and Daniel had their early swim and then went for breakfast on the beach. After that they lazed about and discussed the various spots each had visited. Daniel had booked a special side trip which involved visiting a nearby island. Kay was going to be lazy and maybe have a nap. Arranging to do some scuba diving was also on their respective agendas. They arranged to meet in the dining room of the resort complex for dinner.

Kay was looking forward to her evening with Daniel. He was attractive. He seemed quiet but he had an air of command about him and best of all he did like to dance! She was hoping they would get to dance when the band commenced their nightly efforts. Tonight she was wearing a flowered dress in red and white with splashes of black and yellow. It had a short circular skirt, no sleeves, and the neckline was perfectly simple. She had picked it up on one of her earlier shopping excursions to Eveline Street. She felt really good in it. Her jewelry was minimal. Just David's ring that she had had made into a pendant. You could not tell it used to be a ring but it made her feel good to be wearing it and she felt as if David was closer to her than ever.

There was a knock at the patio door. She went over to see who it was. It was Daniel. "Hi. I decided to walk over and meet you."

Kay smiled. "You look really good." She took in his six-foot two inches. He was solid, no flab, no paunch. The other point in his favor with Kay was that he was not a booze guzzling yahoo. And, more importantly, he could hold and carry on a conversation. He had entertained her and others with stories of any number of escapades and events in his life. He was wearing a light-coloured shirt, Bermuda shorts, sandals, and no socks.

"Come in. I'm almost ready."

"Kay, you look lovely.

"Thanks. I just have to do my pendant and earrings. They won't take long. Help yourself to a drink." She waved her arm at the drinks cabinet and mini-fridge and disappeared into the bedroom. She took a minute to hang up her clothes and place whatever needed washing into the hamper that was collected by the resort laundry service. Everything looked tidy and in its place. She went into the living room-cum-patio and found Daniel had also poured her a drink. Hers was red wine on ice. It was perfect. A short time later they left her cottage for the main dining room of the resort. Their conversation was easy, two people getting to know each other better. She was curious about what he did for a living but really did it matter? Daniel had told her he was going to retire after he got back home. Kay knew from his charmingly accented speech that home was probably somewhere in Scotland. The dinner was perfection! The band played almost non-stop and she and Daniel danced almost every dance. They strolled back to her cottage.

Kay asked, "Would you like to come in for a drink?" Daniel nodded and together they went inside. They sat side-by-side on the love seat. Daniel reached over and brushed his fingers across her cheek and then across her lips. He leaned in and kissed her, lightly at first and when she didn't draw back with increased passion. Kay found she was short of breath. She sat back, gazing at him with slightly parted lips.

Her voice husky, she asked him, "Would you like to stay the night?"

Daniel leaned over to kiss her again and then said, "Yes."

Kay did not really remember how they got to the bedroom or who was in bed first. What she would later remember was the joy she felt being with Daniel. He seemed to fill a void in her soul. A void that had been there for years.

In the morning they took turns showering and strolled up to the restaurant. The plan after breakfast included a short excursion into the mountain highlands. On the train, Kay said to Daniel, "You know, you've never told me what you do for a living."

Daniel looked at her and said, "That's because my profession usually makes people nervous."

"Well, what is your profession?"

The silence between them lengthened and then Daniel said, "I'm an Inspector for the Glasgow Police."

Kay was astounded. Of all the jobs he could have, why did it have to be law enforcement? Her comments and thoughts did not match up. "I'm sure that I am going to be fine about your job. After all, I live in Canada and you live in Scotland. There really shouldn't be a problem, should there?" Her brain was in a jumbled whirl. What was she going to do? She really liked Daniel but he was a cop! Well, it sure wasn't going to be a problem because when they left the island he would go his way and she would go hers. What could possibly go wrong now?

She decided then and there that today was going to be a fun day. The train trip would take three or four hours and their plans included some cave exploring and an underground body of water for snorkelling and scuba diving. Kay intended to do a lot more snorkelling when she got back home. She was fascinated by the underwater world. They parted company late into the afternoon. Daniel told her that he would stop by and they would go to the Christmas Eve party together. Everything was starting later than usual. There would be no need to rush.

CHAPTER 27

The Best Christmas Ever...But

Christmas Eve. Kay's eyes mirrored her happiness. She had never felt so carefree in years. She wore a sequined little black dress with strappy, delicate looking heels. Her jewelry was a druzy agate necklace and earrings with silver accents from Expressions in Beads. She had spotted the set at a Christmas craft show for Craig Street Cats. It was different and it had a primitive look to it and made her feel really, really good whenever she wore it.

The resort had laid on a special program for all their guests. The meal had been outstanding. She enjoyed a totally different salad and her protein was grilled fish caught earlier in the day. Along with that she had a shrimp cocktail and more red wine. Dessert was a triple chocolate mousse with pomegranate sauce and mint sprigs with rolled wafers. Daniel had ordered steak medium rare and a baked potato which had been flattened and topped with cheese and chilies. The vegetables he chose were local to the region. He had ordered the same dessert as Kay and his drink of choice was a light beer. After dinner they went for a walk on the paths that skirted the edges of the ocean and the resort.

Shortly after, they heard the music and headed back into the dining room. The entertainment was absolutely top notch and the two acts that had been booked for the kids were terrific. The oohs and ahhs of the youngsters, their eyes as wide as saucers, almost had Kay wishing she was a kid again. There was a bit of an intermission while parents put their kids to bed or made sure that the older ones had suitable things to watch while the parents would be otherwise occupied. Daniel and Kay chose to stroll about outside. The stars were out in full force and the sky was a kazillion pin pricks of light. It was quiet as they walked along the beach. Daniel commented that the tide appeared to be lower than usual but the walk itself was magical. They slowly made their way back to the dining room that had been transformed into a flower-filled dance floor complete with twinkling lights and the most perfect music for slow dancing. For the first time in years Kay felt that a connection had been made that could last beyond these few short weeks. "Let's just enjoy this. Today has been absolutely magic." Daniel agreed and put his arm around her shoulders as they entered the flowered bower of the dining room.

They stayed and danced and talked and danced some more. Kay told Daniel how she happened to choose Phuket for her Christmas getaway. They stayed until the band began playing *Good Night, Irene.* After the orchestral notes of *God Save The Queen* faded, Daniel walked Kay back to her cottage. They stood on the veranda and looked out at the ocean and the reflection of the moon on the water.

"Daniel, would you like to come in?" Kay asked.

"You know, we've had a really big day and it is late. How

about I come for you early and we have breakfast together. Then we can plan the rest of our day. I'm only here for another four days."

Kay's face did not reflect her disappointment. "That sounds like a plan. I'll see you in the morning." She gave him a hug and watched Daniel walk up the path back to the resort. Then she went inside and locked her door and poured herself a small red wine and sipped it while she got ready for bed. She creamed her face and neck and used her hand therapy cream on her arms and hands. The cream was keeping any dry skin at bay which was really good considering how much time she was spending in the water. She got into bed and was thinking that tomorrow would be here in no time at all and then she was asleep.

It was Daniel knocking on the patio door that woke her up.

"Oh my God, I've slept in!" she exclaimed.

"Not to worry. Merry Christmas! I'll wait for you on the patio. Take your time."

"Merry Christmas to you, too, Daniel. I'll be as quick as I can." Kay really boogied. She had a quick shower and then took a few extra minutes to decide what to wear. She didn't know what Daniel's plans for the rest of the day were but a sleeved top and her walking shorts were probably a good choice. She picked her most comfortable sandals as opposed to the most fashionable ones she owned.

"Hi, there. I'm ready and I'm starving!"

Daniel looked at her. "You are well worth waiting for! Let's go eat and then we can decide what we are doing for the rest of the day." They took the path to the hotel and it was wide enough to walk side by side and at some point Daniel took her hand in his. Kay was aware of an extreme feeling of happiness. It was a feeling she had not experienced for a very long time. It had been years since she had felt so at home and so happy being with someone.

"Have you noticed how quiet it is? I wonder where all the birds have gone?"

"Something must have spooked them. I'm sure they'll be back," was Daniel's reassuring comment. "You know, Kay, how about I check out of the hotel. If you like I could stay these next few days with you. I can always catch the runabout back to the ship from this end. That way, we can make sure we get to spend as much time together as we want. Maybe your next trip could be to Scotland, specifically Glasgow!"

Kay was silent for several minutes and then replied "Yes, that is a definite possibility. There is another option. You could make a trip to Canada and Winnipeg, Manitoba yourself!"

Daniel smiled "Yes, Kay, it is very possible."

CHAPTER 28

The Beginning of the End

Kay was waiting for Daniel to return from the loo. She was checking her beach bag-cum-carry-all. She opened the zipper compartment and made sure her will was there along with the sealed envelope addressed to the detectives in Winnipeg. She dropped her bag on the sideboard and went to stand on the veranda. Where was all the noise coming from? She could hear screaming. Lots of screaming. She turned to call Daniel. And in that instant, Kay's world was turned upside down.

Where had all the water come from? There was so much water. *I'm going to die*, Kay thought. David and Daniel got mixed up in Kay's mind. Her thoughts were jumbled and made no sense. She was able to surface for a few minutes and grabbed some frantic mouthfuls of air before she was pulled under again. She had managed to grab hold of a tough leathery branch. A palm branch! She knew the trees were very tall and the palm leaves were always at the top. How was that possible? She hung on for dear life. All around her was water. Lots and lots of water. Water as far as she could see. She had no idea where she was. She did not know where Daniel was. Then she remembered. He had gone to the loo as he called it. Kay realized she was in serious trouble. She hoped Daniel was safe. There was so much of everything in the water and she had no idea how she was going to get out of this if she ever did. She wrapped her legs around the tree as best she could. Her arms barely made it around the tree trunk. She did not know how long she would be able to hang on! It seemed like hours but it probably wasn't. She saw a small shape bobbing in the water. It's a kid! Kay let her arms unwind and she reached over as far as she was able to try and grab at the child. He was so small. She grabbed a chunk of his shirt, hauled him over to the tree where she hung on for dear life. He appeared lifeless but she found a weak pulse. She pushed on his chest while she held him against the tree and she was soon rewarded with some coughing and sputtering. After several minutes of hanging on to him as best as she could. With some difficulty got through to him getting him to wrap his arms around as much of the trunk of their palm tree as he could. She wasn't sure how long he would be able to hang on. Then she remembered that the belt on her shorts might do the trick. With great difficulty she got her belt off and wrapped it around him and the tree trunk. It just made it. She did not know how long it would hold. She did not know how long they would be trapped so high up. With water all around, there was no way of knowing exactly where they were. There were no recognizable landmarks anywhere that she could see. Everything was under water and only the treetops were visible. The roaring of the water had seemed to subside but she wasn't sure. Every once in a while a body would be swept past them. She knew that it was a body, not a life, and she was wondering how long they would be able to last on their perch. She wished she knew what had happened to Daniel. The nights together were the best ones she had had in years. It really wasn't fair! All this time and finally she finds someone she can be with and be comfortable and at home with and now *this*! Kay spent some time comforting the little fellow. She tried to instill how important it is to hold on to the tree. She did not know for sure if he understood anything of what she told him. She noticed that he was shivering uncontrollably. There was not much she could do but maybe her shirt would help. She was able to divest herself of her shirt and get his arms through the sleeves. Maybe it would help but now she was feeling the cold! The sun was so weak. It had no warmth. Kay was beginning to feel the cold right into her core. Even if the water receded, and it looked like it might be doing that, how were she and the boy going to get down? They were too high to allow themselves to drop down. And if they tried to shimmy or slide down they would probably tear their legs and arms and whatever was bare on the tree bark. "I just need to hang on...hang on...hang on," Kay kept repeating under her breath. She felt the water on her legs. *Oh my God! Where is the water coming from?* She realized that the water that was responsible for putting her in the tree was returning like an out-of-control freight train. It was going to do some serious damage. There was no time to think! She could see the height it was reaching and she could hear the roar of its return. She indicated to the young lad not to let go and that was all the time she had.

When she became aware of her surroundings she was no longer on the tree. She was surrounded by water. She was ready to give in, to let the water have its way, when something bumped against her. She grabbed on to it as best as she could. She did not know what it was but as long as she hung on it would keep her afloat. She took a long look around. "I think...I think...I'm in the ocean!" She could not see any outcroppings of land, just water as far as she could see. Surrounded by water. Water all around her!

Daniel had come out of the loo into the sitting room of Kay's suite. What the hell? Everything was wet. The carpet, the bed, there were even fish flopping on the floor and water. Huge puddles of water! *What's going on? Where's Kay?* He spotted her bag. It was hung up on a branch outside the room. There was no sign of Kay's suitcase. Over in the corner of the room was one of the gifts she had purchased for someone back home. Where the hell was she? Why was it that the entire room looked like it had been inundated with water? Obviously, it had. The fish and all the water were irrefutable evidence.

He left Kay's ID in her wallet but he removed the envelopes that were in the zippered compartment. Neither were addressed to him but one was addressed to the City of Winnipeg Police Department, Attention: Detectives J. Moore and Wm. Jessiman. The other was labeled *Last Will and Testament*. Daniel felt that the letters were better off in his hands. If he could not find Kay alive or even locate her body maybe he would open them or maybe he would just mail them to where they were supposed to go. By rights, he should not even be hesitating but something was holding him back. Suddenly he became aware that the water was coming back into the room. He had been safe in the loo before so he ran back in and worked fiercely to shut the door. He almost did not succeed.

Daniel was forced to remain in the bathroom for what felt like forever but was only several hours. He opened the door when he became aware of voices and lots of shouting and yelling. There was no more water in the room when he opened the door. There were more fish on the floor and most of them appeared to be dead but a few were still flopping about. Kay's purse was gone. The voices he heard had come from outside. Some of the resort staff and local law enforcement were going cottage to cottage looking for inhabitants. No, looking for survivors, probably. Daniel felt very, very cold. This was not good. He waited for the others to get to Kay's cottage. He showed the police person his identification and explained that he and Kay had been together and they had breakfasted together and were getting ready to go out for the day. He had been in the loo and Kay was doing some last-minute packing. They had asked him what she was wearing but he could not remember. He kept silent about the envelopes. He had already promised himself that they would reach their destinations even if he had to deliver them himself. He needed to know what it was all about. But, most important to him now was—where was Kay?

CHAPTER 29

He asked the senior officer exactly what had happened.

The officer replied with some degree of hesitation. "We are not one-hundred percent sure but the word is that we have experienced a tsunami."

Daniel digested this information and then asked, "Would that account for the tide going out further than it has since we've been here and also there were no birds around last night or this morning? It was unbelievably quiet, actually more than quiet, we had total silence outside."

The officer nodded his head in agreement and finally said, "Yes. What you are describing has been mentioned by other survivors. First, the water is drawn back from the ocean for many miles. Once the pressure becomes too much to bear it returns at a very rapid rate and when it finally runs out of steam the water is covering a tremendous area and has come in at an unbelievably strong force and it is also very deep. We have been told that the water was higher than most of the trees around here. After some time, the water seems to recover its strength and it is pulled back towards the ocean and as it goes back it gathers even more speed and force on its return trip. Very few survived this part unless they found shelter in a strong structure that could not be washed away. The mountains did provide some protection but if you weren't really high up it would not matter. We've found fishing boats marooned miles inland but no fishermen. And it appears that there are very few survivors except for those that made it to the highlands.

"If I may review what you have told me. The lady who occupied this cottage was Kay OsbournOsbourn and she was from Canada, specifically Whinneypeg. We will be preparing a list of missing, injured, and dead that can be verified. This is where photographs will play a huge part in the identification process. In this heat, the bodies will not last long. We will also have to be watchful for diphtheria, cholera, dysentery, and other diseases that will run rampant through the remaining population."

Daniel followed the group from the cottage. He tapped the senior officer on the shoulder. "Excuse me sir, could I be of any help?"

"Yes, of course. It is very good of you to offer your assistance. We have a fairly large number of Brits and Scots here for Christmas. This resort is known for its Christmas and New Year festivities. If you like, you can come along with us now, or I can give you directions to the station for tomorrow morning."

Daniel did not hesitate. "I can come with you now. My hotel is on the other coast. If I could get a ride there this evening I would get some clean clothes and make arrangements to extend my stay. Also, I know what Kay looks like. If necessary, I could identify her. I know she did not have her purse with her because when I came out of the room the first time it was hanging from the tree outside her cottage. There wasn't a trace of her! The room was filling up with water again but I took shelter in the loo. I mean the bathroom. I was only able to shut the door using all my strength and using the tub as the stopper for my feet as I tried forcing the door shut. I was in there for a couple of hours for sure. The first time I don't think it was for that long but the second time—that's the first time that I saw anyone else. Her purse was no longer in the tree." The officer waited to see if Daniel had anything else to say but when Daniel stayed silent he addressed Daniel by his official title.

"Inspector Gregor, I am going to send you off with one of my officers. You need some warmer clothing. The next few days are going to be very long. It is quite probable that the weather will get worse." He looked around the group and motioned one of his men forward. "Tomas can speak English so you will be able to converse with him." He spoke to Tomas in their regional dialect and gave him a set of car keys. "I've told him to get a room for the night and he can bring you back tomorrow morning. You are on my expense account for the next little while." Daniel shook his hand, turned away, and departed with Tomas to get the car.

He and Tomas carried on some conversation but Daniel noticed he was really tired and the next thing he knew he was asleep! He slept for most of the journey and awoke when they were about an hour away from his resort on the opposite coast. When they arrived everything was as it was supposed to be. Lots of people. Locals, tourists, birds twittering and squawking and everything as neat as a pin. Nothing was out of place.

He wished that he and Kay had stayed here instead of returning to her resort for Christmas Eve. They had only spent several hours over a couple of days but their nights together had been special. He had enjoyed himself and enjoyed her company immensely. In fact, if truth be told, he had not enjoyed himself so much in years. "I miss you Kay." he whispered.

Daniel and Tomas had supper together and then each retired to their respective rooms. Daniel had contacted Glasgow and his time on the island had been extended by as long as was necessary. He was no longer on vacation. The Thai police were really going to need lots of help. There would be lots to be done before he was able to return home to Glasgow. He packed his bags and paid his bill. They would be leaving in the morning to return to God knows what. In his heart Daniel knew that Kay was gone. Not just lost, but gone. His conversation with his boss replayed over and over in his head. In his conversation with the Super a phrase kept popping into his head. It was from the BBC news, the words "bloody nightmare." His boss had told him that the phrase had been repeated many times. Daniel knew this was not a nightmare, bloody or otherwise. When one woke up from a nightmare everything was normal. Everything was as it was before one went to sleep. Nothing was the same here. Everything was changed. Nothing would ever be the same again. Nothing was normal. He was not looking forward to the next few days or weeks There would be lots of deaths, unbelievable displays of grief, families torn apart, children left without parents and parents who would have no offspring to parent. People with no homes to return to because their homes had been carried into the ocean by the tsunami or beaten to pieces by the incoming and outgoing speed of the water. He wondered if the full magnitude of the disaster would ever be known.

Daniel had placed the two envelopes he had removed from Kay's carry-all in the inside pocket of his jacket. He felt like he had a fire raging in his jacket pocket. He wanted to open both envelopes but he would not. He would deliver the one to the Winnipeg Police himself. But the one addressed to Kay's solicitor—that one he would forward from Scotland with his own cover letter. He suspected, no, he knew. Kay was gone but deep down he was hoping for a miracle.

CHAPTER 30

Daniel Heads for Home

Daniel had opened the letter labeled *Last Will and Testament*. Kay had ordered the farm to be sold in the event of her demise. She had stipulated that the farmer renting the land was to be given first choice to buy the land. She had made some bequests to several charities, her church in Carberry, and to the ESL Department of River College where she had been employed. She also indicated that she wanted to be cremated and her ashes placed with those of David Carter and if that was not possible then with her parents.

Daniel wondered who David Carter was. He guessed he would find out eventually. Actually, he knew he would find out. Kay was becoming more and more topmost in his mind. He hated loose ends. He hated having questioning thoughts and doubts circulating over and over in his head and no way to get answers.

Daniel flew home to Glasgow two months later. The island Police Chief had hosted a get together for him with the officers and other volunteers. It was bittersweet. The vibe in the room and within the group was more relaxed, even a wee bit happier. It would take longer, probably months, but things would improve for everyone left behind. He did not think he would ever return to Phuket.

Daniel retrieved his car from the long-term lot of the Glasgow airport. He would be back to work in two days. He already had an appointment with his boss. There would be lots to talk about. He needed to forward Kay's Last Will and Testament to her lawyer in Brandon, Manitoba. She had still not been declared dead but that would happen within the next couple of months. Her body and dozens of others had never been located. Several bodies had been fished from the sea by nearby islanders who were not in the path of the tsunami but they had no way of knowing where the people had come from so the islanders took care of the details.

Daniel's mind went back to the young lad who had been found at the top of a palm tree. He had been wearing a belt to hold him to the tree and the remnants of a woman's shirt along with his own shirt. He thought the pieces of it looked familiar but he could not be positive. As his state of shock wore off the wee lad was able to share more bits and pieces. The lady had hair like his auntie, very curly and short. She had managed to catch him, strapped him to the tree and had given him her shirt because he had started shivering uncontrollably. He remembered he was very, very cold. They were in the tree and suddenly the water came back...and she was gone. He was all alone until the searchers had found him. Daniel had felt so sorry for the little blighter. He had left some money with the police chief of Phuket to ensure that the little guy was looked after.

Daniel really wanted to open the envelope addressed to the detectives but that had to be done in the presence of his commanding officer. He should have opened it in Phuket but Glasgow would have to do. He would find out what it contained tomorrow.

Daniel woke up early. He decided he would have breakfast at home. He would pick up something for coffee for everyone on his way to work. He remembered something Kay had said about a place called Oscar's in Winnipeg. Instead of muffins or donuts he would get bagels and some plain cream cheese and brie to go with them. He arrived early with twenty minutes to spare before his appointment with the boss. Everyone was happy to see him and he was glad to be back at work. The bagels and cream cheese and brie were a big hit.

He waited in the outer office and in no time the door to the inner sanctum opened and the boss was there beckoning him to come in. They shook hands and he told Daniel, "The men were really happy to hear you had survived. You should have heard the cheer they gave when I told them. So, are you ready to come back to work? Or do you need a bit more time?"

Daniel did not answer but chose to take the envelopes out of his breast pocket and laid them on the desk.

"What's this, Daniel? It is addressed to some detectives."

"Well, sir, I don't know because I have not opened it. The lady I was with prior to the tsunami...they are hers. I found them in her purse before the water came back. I kind of forgot about them for a while. I thought that with everyone busy with what was happening in Phuket there would not be time to deal with them properly. I had intended to fly to Canada, specifically Winnipeg, for my next vacation. I don't know what is in the envelope but I had intended to ask her to marry me." Daniel stopped. He was a little shocked. Until that moment he had not defined the direction of his relationship with Kay. "I did open the Last Will and Testament and it is what it is. I had intended to mail it to the lawyer in Brandon, Manitoba."

His boss looked at the envelopes on his desk. He picked one up and turned it over. "You know Daniel, I do want to open it but if I do there is no turning back. I don't even know if opening would answer any of my questions or yours. If, as I believe, that there was some wrongdoing then we wait for them to come here but if it stays sealed and you deliver it in your capacity as an Inspector, Glasgow Police, you may find out the whole story and I think you need to know the whole story. We'll give you two more weeks. I'll make a note that it is related to the tsunami. We'll see you back here in two weeks."

Daniel thanked the chief inspector and left the station quickly. There was lots to do to be back in two weeks' time. His first stop was his travel agency for a ticket to Winnipeg, Canada, then he would contact Detectives Moore and Jessiman. Once that was taken care of he would rent some form of transportation and drive out to Brandon to drop the envelope off with the lawyer.. It could all be done in two weeks providing the flight out was tonight or tomorrow morning. Daniel's business with the travel agency was accomplished in record time. He was flying business class and the flight was leaving the airport at 2300 hours. He would be landing in Toronto and then catching a connecting flight to Winnipeg. He would contact the detectives when he got there. Once the envelope was opened everything would fall into place, maybe!

CHAPTER 31

Daniel would have liked a few more days at home but two weeks to take care of this was all that he had been given so time at home was shelved. He repacked his carry on—shirts, socks, briefs, several t-shirts, and two pairs of jeans. He would wear his suit. He showered, shaved, and pulled out his fall suit. It was medium gray, his shirt was black, and his tie was gray with black and silver stripes. He wore his brogues because they were better for walking in damp and wet conditions. He thought it was winter where he was going. Daniel arranged for his neighbour to keep an eye on his place. Plus, someone from the department would be assigned to do a drive-by later at night on an intermittent basis. The drive-bys would continue until he got back. Daniel locked his door and got back into his car. It was a matter of turning in the cul-de-sac and then he was on the road to connect with the main highway and off to the airport. The airport journey, including going through customs, was uneventful. He slept most of the way on the flight. When he arrived in Toronto he was well rested. He had two hours to wait before catching his connecting flight.

He would walk around and stretch his legs. He could eat when he reached Winnipeg.

The flight from Toronto to Winnipeg felt like it was over before he had even noticed they were in the air. He had a row of seats to himself. At least he was not bombarded by questions as to where he was from or going to, even, as had happened on another flight, propositioned. That was nipped in the bud when he mentioned he was with the Glasgow Police. He still remembered the young woman's look of consternation which changed to one of worry. He basically told her to be more careful and put his seat back and appeared to doze off. It was not a full flight so it was no surprise that his seat companion was gone when he woke up. He did see her hurrying out of the automatic doors but he was still in line. He knew she would be way more careful about approaching strange men in the future.

The landing in Winnipeg was textbook. He did not have to go through customs as he had done that in Toronto. The nearest hotel was several kilometers away, so he flagged a taxi and asked the driver if he could recommend any one place in particular, preferably within walking distance of the main police station. The driver suggested the Hotel Fort Garry on Broadway or the Winnipeg Inn.

Daniel asked his driver, "Which had the most reasonable rates?"

"Well, sir, I think that would be the Fort Garry. The station is a good walk, about twenty minutes, and it is almost a straight line."

"Well, then, the Fort Garry Hotel it is," Daniel replied.

The driver continued. "You can also get a map from the

front desk and if needed, sir, here is my card. Just ask the dispatcher for me."

Daniel glanced down at the card. "Thank you, Tom." They had arrived, so he tipped the driver, got out, pulled his bag out, shut the taxi door, and waved Tom off. The Fort Garry was a period hotel. He wondered what it would be like. He really would have preferred something a little more modern but he was willing to give it a go. Daniel walked up the staircase and through the revolving doors. Maybe this would be okay after all. The light was subdued. The reception area was off to one side not tucked away but out of the road of all foot traffic. He walked over. "Good afternoon."

"Good afternoon, sir. Do you have a reservation?"

"No. I left Glasgow last night and except for my stopover in Toronto I've been on the move. I hope you have a room available? I'll probably be here for a week to ten days."

"Just let me check, sir. We do have a vacancy on the fifth floor. Room 508."

"Terrific," Daniel replied.

The desk clerk entered his personal details and handed him his two room keys. Daniel thanked her and turned away and headed to the elevator and the fifth floor and Room 508. After settling in his room, Daniel contacted the City of Winnipeg Police Station. Apparently Detective Moore had retired a few years back but Jessiman was now the head honcho of detectives so he should still be able to get some answers. At least, that is what he hoped. Once the appointment was taken care of it would be time to contact the lawyer and deliver Kay's Last Will and Testament to him. There was a finality to this that he was finding hard to accept. His memories of Kay would pass from the forefront of his mind. They would gradually recede, until he would not be able to recall what she looked like.

The hotel itself was very old. It even had the required ghost according to the two young people he had trailed down the corridor who were planning on staying up to see the ghost.. Daniel had lunch in the hotel. The food was outstanding. He had opted for a hot roast beef sandwich with a really good gravy and horseradish, a Caesar salad, and frites. Turns out the frites were actually potato fries and they were sure tasty. Along with his food he had ordered a pot of very strong black tea. After he had eaten he returned to his room for a rest. As he removed his jacket, tie, and shirt, he was beginning to feel like himself. He removed his trousers and hung them over the back of the chair. The shirt, tie, and jacket went over the back of another chair. Then he laid down on the bed and closed his eyes. He needed a rest before heading out to the Police Station. He had not expected to see anyone so soon but he wasn't going to waste any time. Apparently, the station was in an area referred to as The Exchange, whatever that meant. Daniel picked up the phone and asked the operator to call him in an hour.

"Of course, sir. I will call you in an hour."

When the phone rang it took Daniel a minute or two to get his bearings. He was more tired than he thought. "Daniel Gregor here."

"Good afternoon, Mr. Gregor. This is the wake-up call that you requested."

"Thank you, much appreciated." Daniel hung up the

receiver and swung his legs over to the side of the bed. He glanced at his watch. He had just over an hour and forty-five minutes. It would not be a problem. He pulled his jeans, a dark-coloured shirt, and his leather bomber jacket out of his suitcase. He would forgo a tie today. His brogues would do. He tucked Kay's envelope addressed to the detectives into the inside pocket of his jacket. Daniel took the elevator down to the main floor. He inquired from reception as to the direction he should walk to get to the stations. It did not sound like it was any great distance. It was on the cool to cold side but not as cold as it was back home in Glasgow. The walk barely took fifteen minutes and he was expected. He was going to have a seat and wait when Jessiman came off the elevator and was at Daniel's side before he had time to sit down.

"Inspector Gregor, how kind of you to make the trip. I know you were advised that Detective Moore had retired. I have his job now but I've taken the liberty of contacting him and he will be with us shortly. Let's go up to my office and wait for him there." The elevator whisked them up quietly and quickly. Daniel thought that Jessiman had a decent looking office. There were two armchairs, an oak desk with a matching swivel chair, two filing cabinets, and, in a corner, a couple of corner shelves that held several mugs and six short-sided heavy bottomed glasses.

Jessiman cleared his throat. "Jimmy Moore will be with us any minute but if I understand your telephone call that you made earlier today this meeting will concern Kay Osbourn who is believed to have perished in the Phuket tsunami last year." Daniel nodded. He was reaching into his breast pocket for the envelope when there was a knock on the door. Jessiman got up and walked over to the door. He opened it and greeted Jimmy Moore. They shook hands and then Jimmy was introduced to Inspector Daniel Gregor of the Glasgow, Scotland constabulary. Daniel shook hands with Jimmy Moore. He noticed that his handshake was firm without crushing and he had piercing blue eyes. His chestnut-coloured hair was shot with silver strands. He was still trim and appeared to be in good shape.

Daniel cleared his throat. "Before we get into all the details I should probably tell you how I met Kay Osbourn." He paused, blinked, and cleared his throat again. "I met Kay on the small ship that took us from Singapore to Thailand. I spoke with her just prior to her disembarking at Phuket. She was courteous but not overly friendly so I left it at that. I did run into her several times in the space of a week to ten days and we had drinks together one afternoon after we bumped into each other. She was on a tour of the side of the island I was staying on and I ran into her again and we arranged to have dinner together. I think that was the encounter where she decided I was an okay person to do things with. I can't really say she was overly cautious but she was certainly careful. She knew more about me than I knew about her at the time. On thinking back, she was somewhat taken aback by my job. She had asked what I did for a living and I had replied that I really did not want to say because it tended to drive people away. However she persisted and I finally told her that I was a detective inspector for the Glasgow Constabulary. That bit of information appeared to be a bit of a stunner and she seemed to pause and regroup. I do believe she was beginning to trust me. Right now, I'm a little shocked by the envelope addressed to you both. I expect that it will not contain good news but I want to understand." Daniel took the envelope out of his pocket and handed it to Jessiman.

"It is addressed to you, Jimmy. I'm pretty sure she did not know that you had retired. Why don't you do the honours for us ?" Jessiman handed him the envelope and a letter opener. Jimmy pulled the blade along the flap. He removed several pages and handed them back to Jessiman.

"Okay, Bill, I've opened it up. Now it's up to you to read what it says to us. By the way, I think Inspector Gregor needs to stay to hear this too. If you agree that is."

"Thank you, sir." Daniel replied. "If it is fine with Detective Jessiman."

Bill nodded his agreement. "Let's sit down. This may take a while."

CHAPTER 32

What Moore, Jessiman and Daniel Finally Learn…

Dear Detectives Moore and Jessiman:

This letter was written a long time ago and it has been sitting in a safety deposit box in a Brandon Bank for many, many years. When I chose Phuket as my yearly getaway destination I felt that I needed to reread its contents to make sure all the details were clear, correct, concise, and unambiguous. This letter will explain exactly how and when Dr. Maxwell Meddleton met his end. I ended his life. The next several pages will detail it all for you and it will tell you where I threw the knife that I used to kill Dr. Meddleton. As far as I know, it is still there. I took this letter with me this time because leaving it behind did not seem right to me. I know, I have left it behind many times. I do not know why it had to travel with me this time. Now, please go ahead and read the rest of the story.

I am Katherine Elaine Osbourn I was a graduate student at River College and I was a research assistant for the late Dr. Maxwell Meddleton. Inadvertently, I discovered that Dr. Meddleton had performed the series of Session One tests on a young man who I had hoped to marry. Unbeknownst to me, that young man, David Carter, also signed up for the Session Two procedures. I believe that the money from the Session One and Session Two procedures was very important for David, maybe even very necessary, but I did not know why the money was so important. The last time I saw David was after he had completed the Session One work. Some of this explanation is put together after the fact, as you will discover. David did complete Session One without a problem, however, Session Two was another story. He completed four nights of the second session. Then he was gone. I never found out until weeks later that David had jumped off of the Fortune Street Bridge.

My co-worker Janice Cameron asked me to listen to a tape recording from someone in the daytime second session. It was totally different from all the other tapes she had listened to from the daytime portions of the second sessions. The identifying numbers were DB62 and it was then that I realized why I had not seen David for days, even weeks. The tape that Janice Cameron asked me to listen to was David. It was beyond awful to have listened to it. To this day, I believe his experience verged on horror. Janice was not aware of my connection to the subject on the tape. Somehow, I managed to remain calm but as I listened my anger grew and I knew I had to take care of Dr. Maxwell Meddleton. Also, as time passed, I became aware of the human damage that Dr. Meddleton had wrought. I can remember the advertisements in the local papers—the ones where River College asked for the public to come forward if they took part in any research projects involving River College. The reason put forward was that there had been a fire in the research storage area and various researchers were hoping to salvage some if not all of their work. The researchers needed to know who took part so that they could match individuals to the data that had been rescued.

Actually, it took me a while to realize that there had not been any fire and that this was just a ploy to try and save Meddleton's data! It was only later that I found out that this ploy was aimed at locating the outstanding Session Two participants. Once I realized this, I did what I could to help. Not through the police, but with the notes I had made for myself about the participants. Once their stint in Session Two was completed, I was the one who usually escorted them to the incinerator where all soiled clothing was placed to be burned. I can tell you that none of them were very happy regardless of the money they had made. To me they appeared to be in a very fragile, even brittle, state. I was able to track a number of them down with the notes I had made and I did ask them to come forward but to please keep me out of it as I did not want to destroy my opportunity to graduate with a PhD. So, to some degree I'm just as bad as Dr. Meddleton but I don't believe so. I did what I could to help.

I had a switchblade that I had owned for years. I think it was in a box of stuff that I had bought at an auction sale. I remembered some experiments from my undergraduate days. They were experiments done on rats and involved immobilizing them as instantly as possible. Severing the spine or severely damaging it was probably the most efficient way to get this done and it was certainly less messy than cutting the throat. I killed Dr. Maxwell Meddleton between 11:30 pm and 12:10 am Friday to Saturday. I was back in my car and on the road by 12:20 am Saturday.

The following are the details that I wrote down back then.

I parked my car in the loading zone. I used my keys to get into the building and took the elevator up to the third floor and then used the stairs at the far end of the building to get to the fifth floor. I chose the corridor that gave access to the observation room, the pod, and the black room. I climbed the ladder to the observation room and positioned myself behind a very tall filing cabinet which was also behind the outer door to the corridor. Dr. Meddleton could not and did not see me standing there. When he returned to the observation room, he was carrying a cup of coffee and he placed it on his desk and sat down. He put his headphones on his head, turned the tape machine on, and took a sip of coffee—his last one ever. The switchblade was already opened and locked. I came up behind him and pushed the blade into his spinal column and gave it a good twist before pulling it out and reinserting it into the back of his neck. He was not able to move because I had pushed his chair forward against the desk and he was trapped. I left the knife in the back of his neck. I took hold of his hair in both my hands and slammed his head and face into his desktop several times. At least five or six, for sure. There was blood and white bits that looked like pieces of china. I think that those were pieces of his teeth. His coffee cup had been knocked over but the cup was not broken. I left it the way it was, on its side. I removed the knife and wiped the blade on his shoulder. I closed it, pocketed it, and left the same way I came in. There was no parking ticket on my car even though I was illegally parked in the loading zone. I think I have the cold winds of that night to thank for that.

I believe I told you that I drove around that evening without paying too much attention to where I was going. I drove back home to Carberry. I wanted to be somewhere safe. I was not due back until Tuesday for the afternoon students. I could not believe that his body had not been discovered on Monday or even Tuesday morning. So, when I was paged to come and unlock the door for the class that was due to work there that is what I did. I unlocked the door and stepped back so they could go in. I turned to leave and then the screaming began. I turned around and entered the observation area. The rest of this you know from your records. I did have the presence of mind to record the names of the students who were let into the lab. I remember telling you in one of our interviews that I was fearful for the subjects.

To conclude this confession, on my graduation day, the housemother for our residence approached me full of apologies. She was retiring and was cleaning up several cabinets and while going through one of her last piles she found an envelope addressed to me. The name *David* was printed on the back. I thanked her for finding it. After she left I opened it. It was from David and it contained his proposal of marriage and the ring he had bought me. The money for the ring came from Sessions One and Two. That ring is all I had left of David and I never knew it existed until two and a half years later.

Yes, I did attend the Memorial Service for David when it finally took place and I saw you there, Detective Moore, and Constable Jessiman, as well. I don't know if you saw me. I was up in the choir loft. As for Dr. Maxwell Meddleton, I sincerely hope he is rotting in hell. Believe it or not, I did a good deed when I killed him. If I had not done so, how many more people would have suffered untold damages ending in their deaths or the deaths of others? And none of those deaths would have had any explanation.

If you are reading this letter then I have

met my maker. I do not believe I will end up in hell if for no other reason than extenuating circumstances. If this confession clears this murder from your outstanding records, I have a favour to ask of you. Does this confession have to be made public? Even though my parents have been gone for quite some time I do not wish to tarnish their good name.

Katherine Elaine Osbourn
Signed: this 23rd day of November, 1963

(addendum) I have arranged a bequest to River College for the ESL (English as a Second Language) program to provide all students with advice for any research project that involves student participation. It may not stop another Maxwell Meddleton but it should help to slow things down and provide supports for the students involved. I am also putting my money on the new psychology guidelines and the vow that new psychologists must make which includes the words *Do No Harm*.

(addendum) The switchblade is somewhere to the right in the pigpen buried about a foot down. I regret that this confession is so long

in getting to you. I do wish you both every
success.

There was absolute silence in the room.

Jessiman turned to Daniel and asked, "How did you
come by this letter?"

Daniel replied, "I had left Kay packing some of the
items she had bought, such as souvenirs for friends. I was in
the loo. When I got out everything in the room was sopping
wet and there was no sign of Kay. There were fish on the
bed and fish and other stuff on the floor. I saw Kay's purse
hanging from a tree outside the room. I pulled it down and
looked inside. Her wallet was still in the center pocket. I
looked in the zippered section and there were two large
envelopes. I took them out. One was addressed to you both
and the other was labelled *Last Will and Testament*. I put
them both in the pocket of my jacket. I neglected to remove
her wallet. I had no idea where Kay was but it was not
looking good. I ended up having to take shelter in the loo
again because the water was returning. I was stuck in there
for quite a long time. For sure longer than the first time.

"Things were totally upside down in Phuket. I ended
up staying an extra two months to give the local authorities
a helping hand with the aftermath. I kind of forgot about
the envelopes. However, when I got back home I knew
something would have to be done about them and I talked
it over with my boss. He authorized my trip here."

CHAPTER 33

Daniel cleared his throat. "I have a couple of questions for you. What can you tell me about the victim, the college professor? What exactly did he do?"

Jessiman told him that the Session Two research that Kay referred to was directly responsible for at least eight suicides and four to six murders, in addition to the murder of Maxwell Meddleton. One of the victims had been flown back to Winnipeg from Vancouver and to date she had never regained consciousness. She was in a vegetative state. The wife of one of their constables was another victim. However, she had made what could be described as a partial recovery. She was finally back home but still has to have all the lights on when darkness of night descended. In fact, they had a generator that would take over in the event of a power failure.

Daniel shook his head and then said, "If I've understood the timeline of events, it appears that Kay killed Maxwell Meddleton before she knew that David had died. I need to know, how did David die?"

Jimmy Moore answered. "He jumped off of the Fortune

Street Bridge on a night the city had a five-square mile power failure. The entire area was blacked out. Jessiman and Matt Baxter were part of the Search and Recovery Team. They were the team that recovered the body several weeks later."

"I want to thank you for allowing me to stay and be privy to all these details. Is there anything I can take back to my boss, besides what I've heard here?" Daniel asked.

Moore and Jessiman looked at each other. Moore replied without thinking. "We can make a copy of the *Black Room* paper and some of the notes from the consulting psychiatrist, Dr. Jake Kroeker of the Grace Hospital. He was an integral part of the investigative team. I know Lieutenant Jessiman can have everything ready for you for pickup in a couple of days, probably after you get back from Brandon. Leave your contact number at the hotel and you will be notified when the package is ready for pick up. When is your appointment with the lawyer in Brandon?"

"It is scheduled for late afternoon tomorrow," Daniel replied. "I know Kay is still listed as missing and presumed dead. No one knows for sure but it may be that the last thing Kay did or may have done is save the life of a young lad who was found belted to a tree. He was wearing the remnants of a ladies shirt. He described the lady but it really was not much help because I could not remember what Kay was wearing that morning. The closest description he came up with is that she had looked like his auntie. But so far his auntie has not surfaced and they are still looking for relatives for him." Daniel stood up and reached out to shake hands with both of them. "I'm going to try and catch a flight home to Glasgow as soon after I get back from Brandon as possible but I won't go until I have the information package. I really do appreciate the courtesy you have shown me."

Jimmy Moore and Lieutenant Jessiman thanked Daniel for making the trip and Jessiman motioned to Jimmy to stay while he walked Daniel to the elevator. Daniel pressed the button which would call the elevator up to the fifth floor.

Jessiman cleared his throat. "You don't have to answer this, but I get the impression that Kay meant something to you."

Daniel nodded and replied in a soft voice, "I thought she was perfect for me and I still think that."

Bill nodded and added, "I'm sorry you are not getting a better ending."

Daniel replied, "No, it's fine. Kay was basically a good person and if I understand her career path it involved making sure students made informed choices about any research they were going to participate in and part of her efforts involved making sure they were safe." Jessiman nodded. The elevator arrived, Daniel stepped on, and the doors slid closed.

Bill went back to his office where Jimmy Moore, former Chief of Detectives, was waiting for him. Bill came in and closed the door and walked back behind the desk.

"Well, Jimmy, what should we do? Do you think this has to be made public?"

Jimmy shrugged and said, "I never ever suspected her. Never."

Bill nodded. He went on to add, "To tell the truth, I did not suspect her, either. I certainly did not think she was strong enough! Guess I was wrong about that, too. We should make an attempt to recover the knife and then we can close this case. It will only need a couple of sentences, nothing too specific, making sure we don't focus on whom. We can truthfully say that it was a death-bed confession and I'm pretty sure we don't need to identify the assailant but just like you I'm sure glad that this case is finally closed." They both nodded in agreement.

Jimmy got up and asked Bill if he wanted to stop off for a drink before heading home.

Bill nodded and said, "A light beer would go down very well." He picked up the confession letter and place it in his secure drawer and locked it away.

"I'll deal with this tomorrow. I'll have to let the chief know what is going on." They both walked out of the office and Jimmy made sure the door was locked before they continued to the elevator.

CHAPTER 34

Daniel walked around the downtown and back towards the Hotel Fort Garry. He was thinking about Kay. He missed her very much. He got back to the hotel and took the elevator up to his room. He picked up the telephone and asked the switchboard operator to get his boss for him. He repeated the number to her twice. The connection was completed without a hitch.

"Hello, sir, it's Daniel here. I hope to catch a flight back home probably by the middle of next week."

"That's good, Daniel. What if anything did you learn of the situation?"

"Well, sir, I will be bringing an information package with me. Detective Jessiman is going to put some information together including some hard copies of notes from the consulting psychiatrist. I think that will explain everything as much as possible but I can tell you some of it now. The letter to the detectives was a confession for a murder that was committed a number of years ago. The lady I met in Phuket, Kay Osbourn, was the assailant. Apparently, by killing the person she did when she did—well, she probably saved a number of lives. I'll fill you in when I return with the information package. The package and whatever details I have should tie it all together."

"Terrific, Daniel. I look forward to having you back. See you next week."

"Thank you, sir, I will be leaving for Brandon to see the lawyer tomorrow." Daniel advised him.

"O.K. See you when you get back."

"Goodbye, sir." Daniel hung up.

Daniel walked over to the window and peered out, then he turned around and pulled his jacket off. He peeled his shirt off and hung both in the closet alcove. Then he laid down on the bed. He just lay there and thought about Kay. He could not have helped her. He was an officer of the law and he knew where his responsibilities lay. He missed her so much. He knew then that he would eventually return to Phuket sometime in the future but it would not be for a while. His eyes closed and his breathing grew deeper and he was asleep.

Daniel slept for several hours. When he awoke he was slightly disoriented. Then he remembered everything. He looked in his billfold for the card from his taxi driver, Tom. He asked the operator to place the call. A woman answered and said to leave a number and Tom would call him back. While he was waiting for the call back, Daniel was trying to decide if he wanted room service for dinner or did he want to eat in the bar downstairs and then go for a walk outside before it got too late. Or maybe just stop off for a nightcap in the bar before he actually headed for bed. He decided to opt for room service. He could still go for a walk after that and maybe he could stop off in the bar as well.

He ordered grilled rainbow trout and a Caesar salad and apple pie for dessert along with the really strong black tea. He watched the news from across Canada and the local news, as well. His room service meal was pretty damn good. While he was watching the news, his taxi driver, Tom, called him back.

"Tom, I need to go to Brandon, Manitoba tomorrow but I want to come back the same day. Can you help me out or is the distance too far for you to travel? I have an appointment time of 3:30 pm. I expect to be busy for about an hour but no more than two hours."

"Well, sir, the trip itself will take about two and a half hours. I could pick you up by eleven in the morning and we should be in plenty of time for your appointment. I can catch forty winks while you are busy. Is eleven okay with you? By the way, do you want the meter to be kept running or would you prefer a flat rate?"

Daniel thought about that for a moment. "I think a flat rate would be best, Tom. I'll see you at eleven then. Goodnight." Daniel ended the call. Instead of going for a walk, Daniel decided to stay put. He would go for a walk right after breakfast, sometime between 9:30 am and 10:30 am. The taxicab was not due until eleven am. He would write a travellers cheque for the taxi driver and give him a tip separately. But that was all for tomorrow. Right now he was really, really tired. No nightcap for him tonight. It was time for bed. He placed his tray outside his door, set the lock, and headed for bed.

Daniel was up and awake before seven in the morning. He had a shower and then put on his jeans, t-shirt, casual long-sleeved shirt, and his leather jacket. He still wore his brogues. He took the elevator down for breakfast. He needed to have something to eat but not too much. He would not be getting in much walking today. He ordered bacon and eggs and something called perogies and whole wheat toast and jam and coffee. The waitress brought him his breakfast and he enjoyed every bit of it. The perogies were really quite tasty and he had the choice of apple sauce or sour cream. The waitress promised to bring him both so he could decide which condiment he preferred with his perogies. He liked them both but truth be told the sour cream won out. It was the best! Maybe he would have perogies again...maybe.

He left the quiet of the restaurant and headed out the door for a quick walk that involved at least ten blocks up one way, four shorter blocks and then another ten blocks back. He could see the hotel and he would be back in no time at all. He felt pretty good. Tom drove up just as he sprinted up the main entrance staircase. He ran back down.

"Tom, I'll be back in a jiff."

"No problem. The meter is not running. My boss suggested that I start the mileage rate when we get back on Portage Avenue going west."

"Great, I'll be right back." Daniel ran up the stairs again and through the revolving doors. He managed to grab an elevator that was on its way up. He hurried down the hallway to his room, unlocked the door and headed for his shaving bag. His travellers cheques were in there. He had neglected to get them out before he went for breakfast. He checked his wallet. Yes, he had enough cash to take care of anything else. He could get more money tomorrow if necessary. He left his room, made sure the door was locked, and headed back to the elevator. He was downstairs and out the door in no time.

He opened the back door and climbed in, cinched up the seat belt, and said to Tom, "Let's hit the road. You know, I did not know it was going to take as long as you said to get to Brandon."

Tom said, "Well, it is about one-hundred and seventy to two-hundred miles and the speed limit is only seventy miles per hour give or take. We will also have to slow down for small towns. I'll have you at your appointment in plenty of time, sir."

"I'm sure you will, Tom. I guess I will become a scenery person for the next little while. By the way, I take it we are on Portage Avenue West?"

"Yes, sir, that happened when we went around the corner. I've made a note of the mileage indicator. You are on a flat rate now. I can point things out that might be of interest to you on our way to Brandon if that is okay with you."

"Why not, Tom. I'd appreciate it very much," Daniel replied.

So Tom pointed out points of interest both on the way out of Winnipeg and on the way to Brandon. Daniel asked about the significance of the white horse statue and Tom replied that it was a ghost horse that had something to do with Riel and the rebellion of the Métis people.

"Who are the Métis?" asked Daniel.

Tom replied, "They are the product of the union between First Nations women and the French, English or Scottish explorers or voyageurs. If they returned to Europe they always left their native partner behind, most times because they already had a wife back home. The Métis leader, Louis Riel, was hanged for treason in Regina, Saskatchewan. There is talk of clearing his name." Around Virden, Tom noticed that Daniel's eyes were closed and he smiled to himself. *The man really does need some extra sleep*, he thought. He wondered what had brought him all this way. On the outskirts of Brandon, Tom braked slightly and honked his horn. There was no one on the road ahead of them. He was just trying to wake up Daniel before they got to his destination. Daniel did wake up.

"I guess I fell asleep again, Tom. Sorry about that."

"No problem, sir. I think you needed that shuteye. We are almost there." He pulled up to a large old fashioned looking building. Daniel did not know it but it was where Kay had gone to make her travel arrangements. He thanked Tom for the safe and informative ride and said that he would be out in an hour or maybe slightly more. Perhaps Tom would like to have some dinner with him before they headed back to Winnipeg?

"That would be lovely, sir. Thank you very much."

CHAPTER 35

Daniel took the stairs to the second floor. He noticed that the elevator was an old one with iron, mirrors, and glass. He arrived at the room number for the lawyer and opened the door.

The receptionist was there and glanced up at him. "Can I help you?"

Daniel replied that he had a three-thirty appointment. He gave her his name. "Detective Inspector Gregor of the Glasgow Police." She looked surprised but went on the intercom to announce his arrival.

"Send him in please," were the words Daniel heard. She indicated which door he should open and watched as he strode in. He met Kay's lawyer as he walked forward to greet him.

"Well, Inspector Gregor, you've come a long way. I'm George Budsen. What can we do for you?"

"Mr. Budsen, I'm here to deliver this envelope to you. It belongs"—Daniel paused—"belonged to Kay Osbourn, who is believed to have perished in the Phuket tsunami."

"Oh my, I've been worrying about that. Everything here

is up in the air. No one knows what to do. I've basically said that everything needs to be put on hold until she is officially declared dead. I believe she is still listed as missing, is she not?"

"Correct, but my trip here involved a visit with you, Mr. Budsen, as well as the Winnipeg Police. The police part has been taken care of and now I'm doing the Brandon portion and delivering this envelope containing Kay's Last Will and Testament. I'm afraid I cannot share the reason for the Winnipeg Police stopover but it has been taken care of just as Kay wanted."

Daniel was asked again to explain how he came to be in possession of the envelopes. "I rescued them after I found Kay's bag hanging in a tree outside of the holiday chalet where she was staying in Phuket. It was not far from the edge of the ocean."

"Yes, we saw it all on the news. It was horrifying and terrifying all at the same time. At the time, I did not know Kay was there. Her travel agent informed me. The travel agency is upstairs on the fifth floor."

Daniel continued with his explanation. "I put the envelopes in my jacket pocket and then noticed that the water appeared to be returning, so I hightailed it into the bathroom and managed to close the door with great difficulty. I was stuck in there for quite a while. When I heard yelling and stuff from outside I opened the door. There was no sign of Kay. I had left her doing some packing. She had bought items for people back here. We were supposed to go for a day trip after breakfast but instead we got hit by the tsunami. Assisting the local law enforcement added two more months to my stay in Phuket. Then I returned home and shared the fact of these two envelopes with my boss. It was his idea that I deliver them in person. Anyway, here is her Last Will and Testament. The envelope addressed to the Winnipeg Police was delivered unopened. My boss and I did not think I should open it before it was delivered. I did look at the Last Will and Testament while I was in Phuket. But there really was no urgency to deliver it as I know she needs to be declared dead officially. My original intention was to mail it to you with a covering letter but if I was coming to Canada to deliver the envelope to the Winnipeg Police, then the letter for you could be delivered as well." Daniel waited while Mr. Budsen collected his thoughts.

"I appreciate the fact that you have delivered this to me. There is a copy on file but it is always best to have the original. Do you mind if I look it over while you are here? I can get my assistant to get you a coffee or tea, if you'd rather.

"Tea would be fine, Mr. Budsen, thanks."

Mr. Budsen pressed the intercom button and asked, "Chloe, could you rustle up a couple of cups of tea?"

"Of course, Mr. Budsen. It will be about five to ten minutes. I will bring it in to you."

"Thanks, Chloe."

Mr. Budsen spread the pages apart. "Fortunately, Kay updated her will before she left for her winter holiday." He checked each page carefully for signs of any added changes. He murmured as he scanned each page. Chloe knocked on the door and brought in the tea in delicate china cups along with lemon wedges, sugar, and milk. Daniel had his black with lemon. Mr. Budsen had his with milk and sugar. He finished reading the document and folded it up.

"Well, we now know what we need to do. I will be getting in touch with the farmer who is renting her land. She is giving him first dibs on the farm. He may need some extra time to put the financing together. The bequests are not a problem. But until Kay is officially declared dead, things will be complicated."

Just then Mr. Budsen's phone rang and Chloe informed him that it was the Winnipeg Police on the line. He switched to the line they were on and said hello and listened. Then he hung up the phone and said, "That was the Winnipeg Police with a request to search a portion of Kay's farm. They said it shouldn't take more than a couple of hours and they would like me to be present during the search. Do you know what this is all about?"

"No, Mr. Budsen, I don't. When I leave here, except for a stop for a bite to eat, I am headed back to Winnipeg and I'll be on a return flight to Toronto and then to Glasgow by Monday or Tuesday. I will be back at work in a week." Daniel stood up and put out his hand. "Thank you for taking the time to see me. I'm sure everything will be fine. I did not know the Winnipeg Police were coming out here but I'm sure it is their intention to keep this visit as low key as possible. You are right, you know. Everything has been turned upside down by the tsunami." They shook hands and Daniel turned and left the office. He thanked Chloe for the tea and headed out the door. He didn't bother waiting for the elevator but took the stairs.

CHAPTER 36

Daniel paused in the front entrance and looked for the Moore's taxicab that Tom drove. He spotted it midway down the block. He covered the distance and rapped on the window to get Tom's attention. Tom leaned over and unlocked the door.

Daniel climbed in, did up his lap belt and turned to Tom. "Let's find a good place to eat, Tom."

"Right-oh, sir. We'll head uptown to the hotel. I've been told by those in the know that the food is quite good. As long as we are back on the road no later than six-thirty or seven then we should not have any problems. The forecast is for clear skies and falling temperatures. Depending on when we pull out we should be back in Winnipeg by ten-thirty or eleven. It might be a bit earlier or it could be later but we'll see."

Tom drove around for several blocks. He made two right hand turns and one left hand turn. "We're here, sir." They both exited the taxi and Tom locked the doors. Gravel crunched underfoot as they walked through the parking lot. The front entrance of the hotel was well lit and the steps were solid and not iced up. Tom opened the door and motioned for Daniel to precede him. Daniel looked around as he removed his gloves. He and Tom spotted the sign for the dining room about the same time.

The dining room was reminiscent of a smokers club room. The air exchange must be top notch because even though several people were smoking the smoke was not hanging about at chin level. Round oak pedestal tables that could seat two to six people, leather-backed chairs, candles, and sparkling crystal made it a very elegant setting. Daniel and Tom scanned their respective menus. His decision made, Daniel opted for halibut steak, cauliflower, carrots, a baked potato, and coleslaw. For dessert he was having the apple crisp with ice cream and coffee. Tom ordered the same except he had lamb chops.

He remarked to Daniel, "It's been a long time since I had lamb and I really like it."

Daniel responded in kind. "Normally, I would have ordered beef but you know halibut is king and it isn't available year-round and I have it whenever I can. " Their waitress came and took their orders and she also brought them a beer each. Their beers were compliments of the gentleman in the corner. Daniel and Tom both looked in the direction she was pointing. Daniel recognized Mr. Budsen, Kay's lawyer, and he raised his glass in his direction. He and Tom chatted about the trip to Brandon and the upcoming trip back to Winnipeg.

"We'll have to stop for gas before we leave Brandon," Tom said. "I should have gone for gas while I was waiting for you."

"Not to worry, Tom. Everything will all work out." Daniel looked up. The waitress was headed their way with two plates resting on her upraised forearm. Daniel and Tom got down to the serious business of eating. The halibut steak and the lamb chops were done to perfection. But it was the apple crisp that won out. Daniel ordered an extra dessert to go so that Tom could take some home to his wife. Daniel paid the waitress with a traveller's cheque and he left a generous tip. He and Tom left with happy hearts and for sure a full stomach. Their only detour was the stop for gas and then they were on their way back to Winnipeg. Tom marvelled that they had not seen a single deer anywhere near the highway.

"Someone's looking out for us, sir. Coming up against a deer can take your car out and us, too, if we are unlucky enough." A little later Tom noticed that Daniel's eyes were closing. He turned on the car radio and chose CBC for its good listening music and he listened to the music while Daniel slept all the way home.

Tom pulled up to the Hotel Fort Garry just as Daniel woke up from his nap. He and Tom chatted and Daniel got his billfold out and removed two traveller's cheques. He handed them to Tom.

"I can give you change, sir.

"No, Tom, don't bother. I appreciate the time and trouble you've gone to. Here is a little something extra you can share with the wife," and he handed Tom a crisp one-hundred dollar bill along with the take-out container of apple crisp. Tom was speechless. Daniel opened his door, then leaned over and put his hand out to shake Tom's hand.

"Thanks for everything, Tom. By the way, you weren't wrong. This hotel is number one in my book. Thanks for the recommendation." Daniel turned and ran up the stairs. He stopped to watch Tom drive away. He had probably gone over the top with the cash tip but the whole day had gone quite well and soon he would be back home. Back in Glasgow. He had wanted to visit the farm but when he heard that the police would be showing up there the next morning he had changed his mind. Kay was gone and all he had were his memories. It sure wasn't a lot. A couple of weeks and some memorable nights. And, now he had to add the new facts of the Black Room to it all.

He went into the hotel and up to the desk. "Can you recommend a travel agent for me? I'll be needing a ticket to Glasgow. I didn't know when I would be returning, so mine is open-ended."

"Certainly, Mr. Gregor. I'll be in touch with O'Brien's and someone will contact you after breakfast. Did you have a specific departure date in mind?"

"Sunday or Monday coming up would be fine, thanks."

Daniel took the elevator to the fifth floor. He had bypassed the bar again. He'd get something from room service. When he got to his room he noticed his phone was flashing and he picked it up.

"Mr. Gregor, Lieutenant Jessiman called and said to tell you that you can pick up the information package at the station anytime tomorrow. It will be held for you at the front desk of the station. You will need some identification before you can claim it. Also, you will have to sign that you've received the package."

"Thank you, I'll be there after lunch." Daniel replaced the receiver. His thoughts were centered on tomorrow. The travel agency was calling him in the morning but he did not know when in the morning so picking up the package after lunch would work out for the best. And, if his luck held he would be on his way home and back in Glasgow on Monday or Tuesday depending on when he managed to snag a flight.

Daniel hung up his jacket, slipped off his brogues, laid down on the bed, and let himself go back to Phuket and Kay. He realized that there probably wouldn't have been a future for them knowing what he did now about Kay. He also knew he had made the right decision to open the zipper pocket of the carry-all where the two envelopes had been. He realized that for some reason it was important for Kay to own up to what she had done those many years ago. Enduring all the questions and interviews which at the beginning were probably day-after-day and then gradually were decreased in number and frequency over the weeks, months, and years, must have been very stressful for her. He realized that David had an important place in her life and heart but he also believed that he and Kay had made some headway. Certainly, without the murder of Dr. Maxwell Meddleton hanging over her, maybe they could have had a future together.

Slowly, Daniel sank into unconsciousness, as his tired nerves and tired body gave into a deep sleep. A sleep he really needed. At some point in the night, Daniel awoke. He realized he was still in his clothes, so he took them off and crawled back under the covers and was asleep in no time. He did not awaken until after ten-thirty when his phone rang.

It took him a couple of minutes to remember where he was and locate the phone. He answered, "Daniel Gregor here."

"Mr. Gregor, I have O'Brien's Travel Agency on the line for you." Daniel heard the click and a voice came on.

"This is O'Brien's Travel, Mr. Gregor. I understand that you want to depart Winnipeg for Glasgow either Sunday or Monday. Have you come to a decision as to which day?"

Daniel thought for a moment. "Actually, if Sunday could be arranged that would be terrific. Would I still have the same stopover in Toronto?"

"Yes, your stopover is in Toronto as well as one in London before you catch your connecting flight to Glasgow."

"That sounds perfect."

"I will make the arrangements and have the ticket expressed to the hotel for you later today. If you have not received it by 3 pm please call me."

"Sounds good. Thank you very much." Daniel hung up the phone.

Daniel got up and decided to have a bath instead of a shower. Then he would get dressed and go downstairs to have lunch. After that, he would walk over to the station and pick up the package that was being held for him. All he would have left to do was pack and arrange for a taxi to take him to the airport in the morning as soon as he knew the time of his flight. Daniel filled the tub and noticed a product for men on the counter and decided to try it out. He stripped and gingerly put a foot in to test the water. It was a little bit too hot, so he ran some more cold water and tried it again. "Ahh," he sighed, "it's perfect." He stepped in and lowered himself into the water. He let his body go. He relaxed. After about twenty minutes he noticed the water was getting cooler. He added more hot water and completed his bath using a loofah and some goat milk soap. He towelled himself dry, pulled the plug, and let the water out. He rinsed the tub because he did not want to leave anything to dry on the bottom to make cleaning the tub harder than it needed to be for the chambermaid. He left a tip on the bedside table. Daniel was dressed and on his way to the restaurant. He had perogies again, along with a hot roast beef sandwich that had an awesome gravy. He skipped dessert but had a large pot of tea with honey. Daniel signed his bill. Everything would be paid before he went to bed tonight so he would just have to hand his key in at the desk in the morning.

CHAPTER 37

His walk to the station was completed in no time at all. The afternoon was cold and brisk but it was not freezing. He got there in a matter of fifteen minutes. He informed the desk officer that he was there to pick up a package that Lieutenant Jessiman had left for him. He produced his identification, signed for it, and was on his way back to the Hotel Fort Garry. He put the information package in his suitcase and decided to go for a walk. He went south from the hotel to Assiniboine Avenue and walked all the way to the Legislative Building that had a golden statue at its apex. He decided to return the same way because it was quiet. He could hear the birds, ravens and jays while the traffic noise was less noisey than it was on the main thoroughfare. There were fewer pedestrians, as well. By the time he got back to the hotel it was almost dinnertime according to his watch. He checked in at the desk.

"I will be catching a flight early tomorrow morning. I would like to settle my bill tonight if possible. Do you think I can come back and settle up with you around ten tonight?"

"Certainly, Mr. Gregor. I hope you have enjoyed your stay here."

"I certainly have. You have a top-notch facility. Should I be disappointed that I did not see the resident ghost?

"No, sir, she only haunts the corridors at certain times of the year and it is usually very late at night."

Daniel smiled. "Well, maybe that's for the best then. My days of late nights are long gone. I'll be back around ten tonight to settle my account. By the way, I've been expecting some tickets from O'Brien's Travel Agency. Has anything been delivered for me?"

"Just a moment, Mr. Gregor, I'll have a look." He turned from the front desk and went into a back room but came back empty handed. Then he checked his various drawers and trays. Daniel was getting a little anxious but relaxed when he heard the receptionist say, "thank God!" under his breath. He handed Daniel the envelope. Daniel thanked him and turned and walked to the elevator and rode it to his floor. He unpacked his case and decided what he was going to wear in the morning and then carefully put everything else back in with the information package sitting on the top along with the O'Brien envelope.

Daniel was sitting in the easy chair and realized that for some reason he was not tired so he decided that tonight was the night to try the bar out. He picked up his room key, made sure the door was locked, and took the elevator downstairs. He did not have to think about where the bar was. He just had to follow the increased noise level. It was not standing room only but there were an awful lot of people in there with most of them being at least twenty-five years younger than he was, he thought, as well as thinking that twenty-five years might have been a little off—maybe it was more like thirty or thirty-five years younger than he was. The entertainment did not sound too bad and even though it was noisy the vocals still made it above the din. The accompaniment and vocals were really quite good. He ordered a scotch on the rocks and then made his way over to a corner where he had spotted a space that appeared to be unoccupied. He took in his surroundings. The girls, or more correctly, the women, were really quite gorgeous and their dresses were all different. Most of them were very short and as for colours there was lots of black, a velvety gray, some kind of shiny, sparkly gold material, and the usual soft flow of chiffon. Of them all, he thought, the chiffon was the most feminine. A waiter came over and asked if he needed a refill and Daniel nodded.

"Make this one a double and I'll call it a night." The waiter brought him his drink and advised him that he could take it up to his room if he wished. The morning cleaning staff would return the glass to the bar. Daniel nodded and for a while thought about going back to his room but decided to stay and listen to the vocalist who was on stage. He knew that all good things must come to an end and he downed the last of his scotch and headed for his room. Then he decided to take a detour. The gift shop was still open.

He approached the shop assistant. "I need something that will hold some papers that can be secured so it does not come open by accident. I want to carry it on board the plane with me. It will not be in my luggage. It will be a carry-on. Do you have anything suitable?"

The salesperson was very helpful. "We have these." She showed him some leather items that were about twelve by eighteen that expanded a couple of inches and could be secured shut with some downward pressure on the metallic buttons that ran across the top.

Daniel eyed them and said, "I think one of them will do. I'll take the dark gray one with me."

"That will be $78.77, sir."

Daniel took his billfold and counted out eighty dollars. "Keep the change," he told her. "I'll just take it with me." Daniel picked up the leather carry case and headed once more for the elevator.

The elevator slid to a silent stop at the 5th floor. Daniel got out and headed down the corridor to his room. Inside, he opened the information that Lieutenant Jessiman had left for him and he made sure it would all fit in the case. Everything fit perfectly. Now, he would be able to read some of it on the way home and be fully knowledgeable when he was discussing the details with his boss. He was going to wear his leather jacket, so he put his airline tickets in the inside pocket of his jacket. He would not have to look for them in the morning.

CHAPTER 38

Glasgow and Home

Daniel decided he would dress casually for the trip home. With some relief he folded his suit and dress shirt into his case. He knew it would not be long before he was back at work and wearing a suit but it would not be this one. This one was far too nice for the rigors of his job that often was not clean, neat, or bloodless. With everything taken care of he was ready for bed when he remembered that he had said he would pay his bill. He picked up the receiver. There was no waiting.

"Yes, Mr. Gregor?"

"Look I know I said I'd settle my account tonight. I'm still checking out in the morning but I'll come down first thing to take care of it. Can you have it ready for me?

"Certainly, Mr. Gregor. I will have it all ready for you when you come down."

"Thanks, I appreciate that." Daniel placed the receiver back into its cradle. Now, he could unwind completely. He turned on the television and found a documentary channel and let it take him away. He did not want to think of anything. Sometime later Daniel awoke. The television was off air. He turned it off, got up to go to use the loo, brush his teeth, wash his face and then he climbed back into bed. He was asleep in no time.

He was awoken by the telephone ringing. Groggily, he answered, "Daniel Gregor here."

"Mr. Gregor, I thought I should call you. You should be heading for the airport in about an hour and a half. O'Brien's did tell me when your flight was scheduled."

"Thanks, I'll be down in a jiff." Daniel was glad he had had his bath the day before. It would keep him until the hotel in London. He washed and shaved. He had laid out his travelling clothes and was dressed in no time at all. With his suitcase locked and the leather carry case under his arm he headed out to grab the elevator and pay his bill.

At the front desk, Daniel had to wait for several minutes but in no time he was headed out the door to hail a taxi to the airport. There was no time for breakfast. He would grab something to eat in Toronto before he boarded the plane for London. The Toronto leg of the flight was uneventful. The landing was smooth and he marvelled at the giant bodies of water they had flown over. He had not seen them on the flight to Winnipeg but this time he had a window seat and the blue sky, clouds, and water, lots of it, was something to see. The lakes around here were certainly larger than anything back home.

Daniel found a restaurant in the airport food court that seemed to have several appetizing menu items. He did not order a big meal. Instead, he chose some snack foods. Maybe cutting back would be a good idea. He had eaten very well in Winnipeg and Brandon. His layover was three and a half hours and it went by very slowly at first but then sped up. The next thing he knew his flight was being called for boarding. He had picked up a couple of magazines and a newspaper and he had the information package to read as well. Maybe he would have a look at that for a bit and then read the newspaper. He did not think his reading light would bother his seat mate. They were separated by an empty middle seat. Daniel sat and listened to the safety lecture. Once that was over the stewardesses and stewards began going up and down the aisle with the beverage and snack carts. When that activity settled down the inside of the plane took on its own comforting dimension.

Daniel opened up the leather case and took out the information package. He opened the sealed flap with his finger and took out a handful of pages. He settled himself comfortably and began reading the first research paper. The entire paper seemed to be quite innocuous. Next was a printed explanation from the Grace Hospital psychiatrist. Daniel's brow furrowed. There was nothing here yet but there appeared to be a warning of things to come. By the third paper, Daniel was beginning to comprehend a little of what was going on. He was putting what he was reading together with what he had been told by Lieutenants Jessiman and Moore. There were newspaper clippings and lists of names with cause and date of death. The ages were varied but the dates of death were always within two to six months after their participation in the second set of sensory deprivation sessions. Someone had scratched out *sessions* and had substituted *EXPERIMENTS* in full caps.

At that point, Daniel thought to himself, "I think I've

had enough for now. The rest will keep until tomorrow." He put the papers back into their envelope and then back into his leather portfolio, tucked it under his arm, turned off his overhead light, and went to sleep. It was not a deep sleep but it was sleep and when the approach to the London Airport was announced, along with the instructions to fasten seat belts he was happy and relieved to finally be back home. He had managed to get the newspaper read so that was left behind on the plane. His magazine purchases also went into the portfolio. Going through customs would not take too long. His suitcase would be gone through but he had his identification with him and that usually sped things up.

CHAPTER 39

Daniel's trip through customs was completed without incidence. As per usual, his identification and police badge enabled him to clear customs in record time. He inquired at the airport information kiosk if they could find him a hotel for the night. The young man manning the kiosk managed to find him a room at a hotel away from the airport but within walking distance of the city center. At least getting his connecting flight to Glasgow was not going to be a problem. Daniel checked in and before he went up to his room he checked out the dining and bar areas. He was not sure that they were as good as what he had enjoyed in Winnipeg but be that as it may he would make do. The room was clean and without any outstanding characteristics. Really, all he required was that the bed was comfortable and he would find that out soon enough. His room had a bar fridge and he glanced in to see what choices he had. Yes, there were some mini bottles of scotch! He felt he needed a drink but first he was going to read more of the Black Room information. He would get his drink from the bar fridge in a bit.

Daniel read every page that had been included in the package from Jessiman and Moore. When he realized he had finally read it all he breathed a sigh of relief. He was going to need more than one drink to get to sleep tonight. Parts of what he had read had him shaking his head in disbelief. How could this have gone on for as long as it had? He realized that the answers were money and no oversight at all. Dr. Meddleton had been able to do what he wanted to whomever he wanted. Not all the Session Two participants had experienced the same degree of trauma as David and Sheila but they had all experienced varying degrees of mental trauma. It seemed to Daniel that Maxwell Meddleton had decided when he started the sessions for the last set of participants, which included David and Sheila, that everything was going to be different. Really, Kay had done everyone a favour, even if no one knew that their lives had been saved because Kay had dispatched Dr. Maxwell Meddleton. Also, the work Kay had done to get the participants in Session Two to come forward was quite amazing. The police had not suspected that anyone else was pulling the strings in the background.

He remembered the letter that had been read aloud. She had asked that the confession not be made public to save her parents' good name. Well, as far as Daniel was concerned, she had saved many people including the youngster back in Phuket. He remembered his time at the resort and interviewing survivors. They had described the power and force of the water coming in and how it was so much more powerful going back out to the sea. Kay had not been in the loo or in a room with a closed solid door like he had been. She had been standing in the room that opened onto the veranda and the view of the ocean. She had not stood a chance!

He put the materials away in the portfolio. He kept the magazines out and decided to have a drink before going down to get something to eat. He would probably have another drink when he got back. In fact, the thought crossed his mind that he might need two or three before he would get to sleep. Daniel had fish and chips along with a dark ale. He would have like a salad but the ones he saw coming out of the kitchen did not inspire him to try them out. On the way back to his room he stopped off at the gift shop and purchased several dark chocolate bars along with a bag of salted raisins and nuts. That would keep him until morning and breakfast.

Daniel stretched out on the bed in his skivvies. He had a glass of scotch on the night table, along with one of the chocolate bars that he had already started on. He put the bag of raisins and nuts aside for the last leg of the trip home. He had a magazine open across his legs and was perusing the table of contents to see why he had bought it. About halfway through there was a column heading about research being done to acclimate sailors to the rigors of submarine life. Interested, he remembered that Bethesda Naval had been involved somehow in the Session Two experiments. He tore the page out and put it in the leather portfolio. He would add it to the other information. Daniel decided that he had had sufficient alcohol consumption. He washed his face, neck, chest, and arms, brushed his teeth, turned out the lights and walked carefully back to the bed in the dark. He burrowed under the blankets and hoped that he would be able to fall asleep. He kept the television on the documentary channel and in no time was fast asleep.

He did not stir until morning. He had time to have a decent breakfast. He even did a bit of shopping at the biggest and best department store in London, Harrods. By 4 pm he was back at the airport and boarding his flight to Glasgow. He had called ahead for his car to be brought out of long-term parking and parked within walking distance of the airport concourse. The keys would be locked in the glove compartment. He had a spare set with him. The London to Glasgow flight was accomplished without incident. Daniel had dozed off but woke up shortly before the instructions for landing were given to the passengers. The line for leaving the plane seemed to take forever to get through into the airport proper. Finally, Daniel was on his way to the parking lot to get his car. He pulled his suitcase behind him and carried his key and leather portfolio in his other hand. He unlocked the door and then went around to the back and opened the trunk. He put his suitcase and portfolio in and slammed the lid shut. He walked back to the driver's side and got in. He was beginning to feel that he was finally home. It had taken some getting used to driving on the wrong side of the road back in Winnipeg even though he had been the passenger not the driver. Finally, he saw his road up ahead. He was almost home. He drove into the cul-de-sac and parked, retrieved his cases from the trunk, walked up the path to the front door, unlocked it, stepped in, and shut the door behind him. He left his suitcase by the door. It could get unpacked later. The boss would be expecting him to report in the morning. He had decided on the drive home to stop off in the morning and buy bagels and cream cheese and brie for the guys. The bagels had been a big hit the last time.

Daniel slept through the night. Nothing disturbed him until his alarm went off at 6 am. He reached over and pushed it down so the ringing would cease. He lay there thinking of everything and nothing. Well, lying in bed was not going to solve anything. He needed to get a move on. The boss would want to have a look at the information package for the Black Room and Daniel knew he was going to have a lot of questions. He hoped he would be able to answer them.

Just like before the bagels and cream cheese were a big hit. He met with the chief and gave him the information package to read. "Whenever you're ready, Chief, I'll be around to answer your questions."

"Thank you, Daniel. Perhaps you could arrange some time for me around 3 pm. I'm going to read up on this now. After that we will have things to discuss. Just not this information yet but some additional information that has come to light that has been forwarded to you care of this office."

Daniel was a bit perplexed. Other information? What could that be all about? Well, he would find out soon enough. He went back to his desk and was brought up to date on the outstanding cases by his partner. They divided up the workload and Daniel went off to question some witnesses and get their statements into the official record. He had grabbed some lunch and thought to check the time.

He had half an hour to get back to the station and his appointment with the chief.

CHAPTER 40

Daniel made it back to the station with time to spare. He grabbed a black tea at the kiosk and loaded it with sugar. He smiled after the first couple of sips. It was really strong. Just perfect. He carried it back to his desk and sat down and wrote up his notes from his day's work. His telephone buzzed and he picked it up. "Gregor here."

"Inspector Gregor, the chief can see you now."

"I'll be right up," Daniel replied. Daniel put his tea aside, put his notes in the desk drawer and headed upstairs to see the chief. His assistant nodded in the direction of a very large set of mahogany doors.

"He's expecting you. Go on in." Daniel nodded his thanks and strode forward. He knocked lightly before opening the door.

"Daniel, come in. Close the door please."

Well, something is up, Daniel thought to himself. Usually the door was kept not wide open but ajar. That was so the chief's assistant could knock, enter, and announce that "the chief was expected elsewhere immediately." Daniel closed the door and strode forward. The chief glanced up from the papers he was reading and nodded to the chair that was to the right of the desk. It wasn't right in front but more to the side of the desk. Everyone in the station knew that where that chair was placed indicated the degree of excrement one was going to be in. So, not in front was good.

The chief sighed. "Well, Daniel, I've read the information that you brought back with you. We will discuss it all but not right this minute. I have some papers here that were delivered while you were in Canada. They are for you but came addressed care of me and I think that is because I'm the commanding officer. I think you should read them over and then we can talk." He handed Daniel a thick package of pages. "Take your time. I don't think it is good news."

Daniel began reading the first page and then flipped it up to see whose signature was at the end. It was from the Thai police captain in Phuket whom he had assisted after the tsunami. He kept reading and several pages further his relief that Kay was alive changed to an aching sadness. There were photos that a photojournalist had taken several months previous. Most of the shots were done with a telephoto lens but the facial details were clear and it was definitely Kay.

In the letter, the captain explained that government personnel had not made it to this island in the immediate aftermath of the tsunami. There were so many pressing situations to attend to and if any of the offshore villages required assistance they managed to get a message to authorities. No one from this island had contacted them. The photojournalist was part of a group that had arrived to document things and perhaps raise some funds for medical supplies. The reason all the pictures were taken from a distance was that the islanders were very protective of this woman. They had found her on the beach and she was near death. With careful nursing and attention from the islanders, Kay was brought back to a fragile state of being. Anything could set her to fleeing into the ocean or into the forested areas. The villagers made sure she was kept safe and that she would not need to run away into the ocean where she would not survive. It was believed that this Phūhȳing phiw khāw, this white woman, was there because of the tsunami and it was the villagers duty to look after her until it was time for her to leave. Also, by taking care of her, including feeding and clothing her, they would be fulfilling their duty. Kay was treated as a living deity.

The villagers took excellent care of her. She was alive! Daniel did not know how this was going to end up. The chief already knew that she had committed murder! Daniel's anguish was beginning to overtake him.

The chief glanced up at Daniel. "Keep on reading, Daniel. You need to know it all."

Daniel kept on reading. A sudden severe storm had panicked Kay and she had gotten lost. By the time she was located by the islanders she was in a bad way. They did everything they could but Kay passed away. There was no autopsy done but the authorities believed that it was a virulent strain of pneumonia. When the Phuket police captain showed these pictures to the wee lad who had been rescued from high up in the palm trees he had identified Kay. One minute she was with him and then she was gone. The youngster said that the pull and force of the water was very great and it was her belt that kept him safe. Kay, however, did not have anything to hold her to the tree and that same force carried her away. More than likely she was able to latch on to some debris of some kind and that was what helped her to survive in the water. She was not rescued by anyone in a boat. She was found on the beach, very badly sunburned and dehydrated. It was touch and go for many weeks until they managed to stabilize her. The islanders knew she wasn't one of them but they believed that it was their purpose in life to save her if at all possible. How she came to be there was not their concern. They knew she was from far away. They believed she had been delivered into their care by the tsunami. They had been spared the destruction of the tsunami. The Phūh̄ying p̄hiw k̄hāw was very sick. They needed to look after her and make her well in order to be spared from another tsunami. So, no one reported a white woman to the authorities. It turned out that the pictures the photojournalist took helped identify Kay. When the youngster was shown the pictures he identified her as the lady who had given him her shirt and belt. The resort still held Kay's passport so the pictures were compared and thus Kay was identified. When the Phuket police captain went out there he was too late. Kay had succumbed to pneumonia. She had been interred on the island in the same manner as the locals. The only difference was that her gravesite always had fresh greenery on it. The Phuket police captain included a necklace Kay had been wearing—the ring from David made into a pendant.

Daniel held the pendant in his hand. He was astounded. Kay had been alive while he was still in Phuket. He knew it was probably for the best because he would have had to arrest her. At least he was spared that. He was glad that the young lad had identified her from the photos. Only he, the Winnipeg Police, and his chief knew that Kay had murdered Professor Maxwell Meddleton. Daniel thought it should stay that way.

The Thai police captain also informed Daniel that no family had yet been located for the lad and they were looking for more distant relatives but were not holding out much hope for a happier resolution. He reported that the youngster was fitting in quite nicely with the family he had been placed with. He also thanked Daniel for the money he had left for the youngster's care.

CHAPTER 41

There Is No Never...

Daniel put all the pages together. The chief sat back in his chair and asked Daniel, "What do you want to do?"

Daniel shook his head as if trying to get rid of an unwelcome pest. "Well, sir, as far as I know she is going to be declared dead. I can forward this to the Winnipeg Police or directly to her lawyer in Brandon. Actually, the lawyer would probably be best. Perhaps I could copy the pictures before sending them off. At least I now know what happened to her. I'm grateful that she was well taken care of and am really happy that she has been identified. I know my job would have made for some uncomfortable times had she survived, especially after I learned of the contents of the Winnipeg Police letter. But I am curious, why did the Phuket police captain forward the pendant to me?"

The chief cleared his throat. "You need to read these two pages Daniel." He reached across his desk to give Daniel two more pages.

The Phuket captain thanked Daniel for all his help during the difficult days after the tsunami. He then went on to tell Daniel that he had seen him searching the bulletin boards every morning and every night. He never asked him why but he remembered that Daniel had told him that he and Kay had been spending time together and had been together prior to the tsunami hitting the island. As he was reading Daniel began to tear up. "Inspector Gregor, Kay was holding the pendant when she died and she kept repeating your name until she died."

The chief inspector cleared his throat. "Daniel, we will talk about the information package but we'll do it later in the week. I think you need some time to digest this. I know it has been a bit of a shock for you but there was no other way to do this."

Daniel stood up. "Can I keep this for the time being? I will forward the portion about the identification to her lawyer."

"Of course, Daniel, and make sure you make some copies of the pictures before you send it off and keep the last two pages for yourself. You do not need to send those off. They are yours to keep."

"Thank you, sir." He turned to leave. "I'll see you tomorrow." Daniel opened the door and left. The assistant had left for the day. He walked slowly down the hall to the elevator, the pendant still in his hand and the papers from Phuket held against his chest. He got back to his desk and the room was near empty. The next shift would be coming in soon. He put the pendant in his shirt pocket and parceled up everything else and left the station. He needed time to think, time to be alone, and time to grieve what he and Kay had missed out on.

Things at work heated up for Daniel and his partner

and it was several weeks later that Daniel put the parcel into the mail to be couriered to Brandon, Manitoba from Glasgow. He included a short note to Mr. Budsen. Work went on. Daniel went on. Every day was different but the same. His work was no longer his prime motivation for being. He penned a letter to the Phuket police captain and asked about the youngster. Had they found any family as yet? How was he doing? He again included a bank draft to be put towards the youngster's care.

Two years later, Daniel was on the runabout returning to Phuket. He had retired and he had rented his place. A good friend would keep an eye on things and make sure the rent was paid on time. He wasn't sure how long he would be in Phuket. He did want to visit the island where Kay had spent her last few months and he also wanted to see how the youngster was doing. He had brought the pictures that the photojournalist had taken. He had them professionally duplicated and framed. He still had the pendant. He kept it in his suit jacket pocket. It did not matter that he had not given it to Kay. What mattered was that Kay had been saying his name when she died. That meant something. He meant something to her and that was all that counted.

He had decided to return to the side of the island that had experienced the tsunami. According to the police chief, things had not yet returned to normal. Tourist traffic was slowly returning but not in the numbers they had enjoyed before the tsunami and for a place that was dependent on tourists that was not good. In the event of another tsunami a warning system had been installed but it did not cover the entire area as money had run out. Money was always running out.

A few days later Daniel and the Phuket Police Captain went to see the youngster. He was staying with a family that had connections to the Captain. He appeared to be doing very well. He remembered that Daniel had been there helping everyone after the tsunami and he thanked him for the money he had sent for his care. They had a really good visit and Daniel promised to return.

He arranged for a trip to the island where Kay was interred. It was as the police captain said. Her gravesite was separate from the others but it had fresh greenery on it and there were even flowers. He sat down on the sand and gazed around.

"You know, Kay, you couldn't have picked a nicer spot to settle in. I will probably be returning to Glasgow in about six months but in the meantime I will be back and forth from here to Phuket. I think I may even bring the little guy you saved with me. I think he would like that. They still haven't been able to locate any family for him. It's tough. He's going to school and he is learning to speak English! I expect that in a few weeks we'll be able to carry on a somewhat basic conversation. I suppose I could also learn some Thai but you know that saying about old dogs and new tricks." Daniel smiled and blinked his eyes several times. They were wet. "I miss you, Kay, but what I really miss is what we didn't get to have." He stood up.

"I'll be back." He turned and walked back up the beach to where the boat that had brought him was waiting for him.

The End

The Truth Behind
The Black of the Room

The scientific experimentation behind sensory deprivation is real. The modern day practice of research projects needing ethical approval before experimentation can begin is a direct result of the immense damage caused by sensory deprivation experiments. While this novel is ultimately a work of fiction, it is rooted in truth.

For further information on sensory deprivation research, the following articles are a good starting place:

The Effects of Age on Critical Thinking Ability. Celia M. Friend, M.A. and John P. Zubek, Ph.D, J. of Gerontology, 1958, 13:407-413.

Effect Of Severe Immobilization Of The Body On Intellectual And Perceptual Processes, John P. Zubek, M. Aftanas, S. Kovach, L. Wilgosh and G. Winocur. Canad J. Psychol. 1963, 17(1): 118-133.

The Isolation Chamber: Intellectual and Perceptual Changes During Prolonged Perceptual Deparivation: Low Illumination and Noise Level. John P. Zubek, M. Aftanas, J. Hasek, W. Sansom, E. Schludermann, L. Wilgosh, and G. Winocur. Perceptual and Motor Skills, 1962, 15(1): 171-198.

Personality Characteristics of Successful and Unsuccessful Sensory Isolation Subjects. J. Hull and John P. Zubek. Perceptual and Motor Skills, 1962, 14: 231-240. Research Supported by Defence Research Board of Canada, Project No. 9425-08.

Intellectual Changes During Prolonged Perceptual Isolation (Darkness and Silence). John P. Zubek, Wilma Sansom, and a. Prysiazniuk. Canad. J. Psychol., 1960, 14(4): 233-243.

Behavioral and EEG Changes After 14 Days of Perceptual Deprivation. John P. Zubek. Psychonomic Sciences, 1964, 1(3): 57-58.

Perceptual Changes After Prolonged Sensory Isolation (Darkness & Silence). John P. Zubek, Dolores Pushkar, Wilma Sansom and J. Gowring. Canad. J. Psychol, 1961, 15(2): 83-100.

About Anna Stein & Acknowledgements

Early on in high school I entertained my friends with my stories, and prior to starting up the long road of writing I was busy being a daughter, wife, mother, administrative assistant, and secretary. Most of my working career was spent as a secretary to several physicians and one cancer epidemiologist, and ending up as a secretary in the Department of Psychology at the University of Manitoba. I became a mature student at the U of M. One of the classes I enrolled in was Kate Bitney's Creative Writing Class. The original title for the assignment was *Murder by Sensory Deception* and over time it morphed to *The Black of the Room*.

The research journals I accessed for my information have all been acknowledged. I worked on my story on and off over several years. With friends and some relatives asking me when would it be finished? Prior to 2019 I was probably more than halfway through and trying to decide what was going to happen to Kay. The first COVID-19 lockdown gave me the impetus I needed and I got busy and finished it in 2020. There are a lot of people to thank, specifically Doug and Marilyne for their editing efforts, Margaret for the information on the Tsunami, as well as Brenda in BC for her fine eye. There are others to be thanked from early on and they are Rehman Abdulrehman and Beth Tait. I had lots of encouragement from my professors in the Psychology Department, especially Dr. Tammy Ivanco and Dr. L. Murray and Dr. Ron Niemi. Thank you everyone. The Italian text in chapter one is from the late Vince DeLuca, husband of Dr. Rayleen DeLuca. Thanks to the two staff in the department who showed me the pod before it was dismantled. You know who you are. Thanks to all who kept my boots on the ground and working to finish this. Last but not least, thanks to Douglas, Tracy, Deann and Erin and Doug's Mom, Mary and my parents Dan and Wilma Bobyn.

Manufactured by Amazon.ca
Bolton, ON